=====

Rule Thirty-Four: Sometimes good luck accomplishes more than hard work.

"Well, don't that beat all!" Cowboy said, staring across the two-lane highway at the tacky drive-in. I looked too and saw the black Harley at the same time the rider had spotted us.

He had pulled off the road onto the gravel drive-in lot before he saw us. When he gunned the bike, he nearly lost it. He did a tight U-turn in front of a Chevy with a roof rack and roared back the way he had come.

I pushed the reluctant Mustang up through the gears while Cowboy knelt on his seat and rummaged through his soft sports-bag on the backseat. "How 'bout that, Rafferty?" he said. "We in business after all!"

=====

RAFFERTY'S RULES

W. Glenn Duncan

FAWCETT GOLD MEDAL • NEW YORK

A Fawcett Gold Medal Book
Published by Ballantine Books
Copyright © 1987 by W. Glenn Duncan

Library of Congress Catalog Card Number: 87-90777

ISBN 0-449-13160-2

Manufactured in the United States of America

First Edition: August 1987

For Val, who never stopped believing it would happen.

PROLOGUE

Excerpt from a statement dated June 11, 1970, by Mrs. Wilma Tunney, age 53, of 1123 Oakdale Lane, Richardson, Texas.

. . . and he pointed a gun at me and said he wanted the money from the cash register. I should have given it to him, but for some reason—I don't know what I was thinking—I slammed the cash drawer shut, pulled out the key, and tossed it back into the kitchen. Through the food service port over there. And I screamed. Did I ever scream! Phil—he's the day manager—said that was dumb. I guess he was right. The guy might have shot me. Instead, he . . .

Excerpt from a statement dated June 11, 1970, by Mrs. Jeanne Philmott, age 31, of 5489 Gaston Avenue, Dallas, Texas.

. . . my Gina's tenth birthday, so I took her and four of her friends out for hamburgers. While we were waiting for the food, the Mollison girl—Vivian—excused herself to go to the bathroom. Vivian is such a polite little girl. I wish my Gina had nice manners like that.

After Vivian left the table, I heard a scream. That short woman was over by the cash register. She had her

1

hand over her mouth, like she had said something she shouldn't have.

There was a very tall, very thin man by the cash register, too. He had on dirty jeans and a long-sleeved shirt. And he had an odd gun. It sounds silly, I guess, but it looked like a pirate gun. Not exactly, but sort of . . . Look, I don't know anything about guns. You better ask somebody else.

Anyway, the man's face was gray—he looked like he was sick—and he had long, greasy hair that whipped across his face when he jerked his head around. He seemed very excited. Or nervous.

I was terrified. Especially because of the kids. It's such a big responsibility to take other people's children out in public these days. Who can tell what terrible thing will happen?

After the cashier screamed, people all over the restaurant noticed the man with the gun. Well, my heart almost stopped when I saw little Vivian walk toward that lunatic on her way to the restroom. I tried to call out to her, but my voice wouldn't work.

I don't think Vivian realized there was anything wrong. She just kept walking. Then, when she passed the skinny man, he grabbed her and pushed the funny gun up against the side of her head.

All I could think of was—how will I ever explain this to Marge?

Excerpt from a statement dated June 11, 1970, by Willis Washington, age 27, of no fixed address.

. . . sittin' at the counter, scoffin' down a burger, when this junkie stumbled in and tried to hit the joint. The dude was wasted, man, totally wasted. Hey, who else but a spaced-out junkie would hit a place like this? At noon? With people coming and going all the time?

And that old bag at the register—the one who sneered at me when I came in—why, she was as dumb as the junkie! 'Stead of handin' over the loot, that stupid old mama locked up the register and started screamin'.

Hoo-ee, I figured we was in for a hot session! The dude had him an old shotgun he'd cut down to 'bout so long and he looked crazy enough to use it. Damn gun was a single barrel. With the hammer stickin' out, you know? Not a pump or automatic or nothin'. So the junkie only had one shot coming to him, but, hey, you cut loose with even one big boomer from a scatter-gun like that and there's gonna be teeth, hair, and eyeballs all over, right?

The junkie's eyes was poppin' like they was fixin' to come right out of his ugly face. I wasn't none too happy. No telling what that turkey might do. I figgered he'd shoot somebody. He already showed he wasn't too smart. Soon as he seen he wasn't gonna get no bread, he shoulda run, but he din't.

Dumb junkie. He din't move toward the door or nothin'. I don't think he knew what was happenin'. 'Course, you can't never tell what a junkie's thinkin'.

Or not thinkin', is more like it.

Anyhow, 'stead of runnin', he grabbed hisself a little blonde kid, and he backed up behind the counter mebbe thirty feet from where I was. Then he started hollerin' how he was gonna off the kid, lessen everyone stayed still and shut up.

Me, I was sittin' there, trying to look small, chokin' on that damn hamburger. 'Cos it got hard to swallow, see?

Then a white guy two stools down stood up real slow and easy-like.

Damned if *he* didn't have a piece, too!

The white guy's gun looked like a .38, which ain't much compared to a sawed-off shotgun. Being outgunned didn't seem to bother him, though. He wrapped both hands round that .38—like they do on the TV— and he looked at the junkie. And he didn't say nothin'.

Afterward, somebody said his name was Rafferty. Man, that dude was cool! He jest stood there and pointed his piece at the junkie.

Now, I wasn't too whipped up 'bout that, 'cos I figgered if the junkie decided to shoot that Rafferty honky—why, there wasn't no way he could miss me, what with Rafferty and me being so close together.

The junkie finally woke up to what was going down. Hoo, my, didn't he come on strong; jabbering away sixty to the dozen 'bout how he was gonna do for the kid 'less Rafferty put his gun down, and he'll kill everybody in the joint, and like that.

Rafferty—he don't say nothing. Not a peep. He stayed locked on to that junkie and you can tell he was waiting.

I was waiting, too, wondering which one of them crazy sumbitches was gonna get me shot.

The junkie tried to hide behind the little girl, see, but he too tall and she too small for that. He had one arm wrapped around the kid and he kept that sawed-off shotgun squoze up against her head. You could purely smell how scared he was.

Well, the junkie was hollerin' and the little girl was cryin' and people was ducking under tables. Man, it was like being between Steve McQueen and the bad guys, you know?

This Rafferty, he don't pay no attention to none of that. He jest locked onto that snowbird and waited for his chance.

Finally, the junkie couldn't take no more and he made his move.

Soon as that shotgun moved from the little girl's head toward Rafferty, it all start happenin'. Man, they was some heavy shit going down!

Rafferty, he got off two shots real quick—bam-bam!—like that. The shotgun went off, too. That's why that big hole in the door over there.

I doesn't remember exactly what happened next. Dumb old bitch of a cashier been tellin' folks I fainted, but that ain't so. I was only chokin', see, trying to swallow that crummy hamburger . . .

Excerpt from a statement dated June 11, 1970, by Vivian Mollison, age 10, of 64 Rosemont Avenue, Oak Cliff, Texas.

I like Mr. Rafferty a whole lot.

When the smelly man wanted to hurt me, Mr. Rafferty shot him. Daddy says it's awful bad to shoot people, except it was okay this time, because of "special circlestances."

After Mr. Rafferty shot the bad man dead, I threw up.

Mrs. Philmott cried a lot. Later on, Mommy cried, too, when the policemen told her about it. Daddy didn't cry. He almost did, though, especially when he shook Mr. Rafferty's hand for so long.

Gina's birthday party lunch wasn't very much fun, but I didn't tell her that.

I want to marry Mr. Rafferty when I grow up.

CHAPTER ONE

George Mollison had not changed much in fifteen years; he was still stocky, with a square face and faint freckles. His eyes were still pale and green. He still had a crewcut. Well, at least he had the eighties version of a crewcut.

And he still looked a lot like John Glenn.

There were some changes, though. I remembered George Mollison as a stammering, grateful engineer who had difficulty putting together a coherent sentence. Now, he was calmer and more self-assured. His greeting had been politely effusive. And he was heavier—weren't we all?—and better dressed. George's clothes were rich-casual; a yellow polo shirt over tan linen trousers, and he had a gold Piaget wristwatch worth more than my car.

My wardrobe was hired-help-casual. I had a polo shirt, too—without the designer's name above the pocket—and faded jeans, and my watch was a thirty-dollar Casio from Zales.

We sat across from each other at a white wrought-iron table, facing away from the house and the early summer sun. A young Hispanic maid with deep, liquid eyes served me vodka on the rocks, and garnished it with a shy heart-breaker of a smile. I wished for a rose to give her. She left, I sighed, and George and I settled back in the patio chairs to survey his kingdom.

Kingdom was the right word. You could have commissioned a fair-sized castle for the cost of property in that part of Highland Park. And had enough left to stock the moat with a goodly selection of prime dragons.

The big house behind us was brick, painted white, and it whispered *money* with every invisible brushstroke. In front of us, a flawless lawn dropped away from the flagstone patio like a bright green bridal veil; the lawn oozed around the tennis court and lapped at the swimming pool, then stretched a long way toward the horizon. A *long* way; about a hundred thousand dollars worth.

"Not bad," I said. "Did the other guys on the armored car heist get away, too?"

"What?" George said. "Sorry, I didn't catch that."

"Never mind. Just admiring the real estate."

"Oh. Yes. Well, in some ways, we have been fortunate."

"No kidding."

George ignored me. He stared without expression at the tennis court. Two women, crisp and sterile in white outfits, batted the ball back and forth. Even at that distance, I could see the younger one didn't have her heart in the game.

"Is that your daughter?"

"Yes," he said.

"All grown up now."

"Yes," he said again. "Vivian is twenty-five now. Thanks to you."

While I made modest "it was nothing" noises, Vivian Mollison glanced toward us. George clamped his mouth into a broad, phony grin and waved to his daughter. She turned her head away without responding and George's grin disappeared as fast as it had appeared.

"Rafferty," he said, "I need your help."

"Oh?"

I had wondered why he called me. George Mollison playing face-from-the-past time hadn't rung true.

Now it sounded like he was one of those rare and treasured blessings—a rich client. In which case, he would ramble for a while, avoiding the unpleasant task of saying the words. People often do, when they hire a man like me.

"I should have kept in touch with you," he said.

"No need."

"You left the police force."

It wasn't a question, so I didn't answer.

"Why?" he asked.

That seemed to qualify as a question. "I don't look good in blue."

"Seriously," George said, "why did you quit?"

"I didn't quit," I said. "I got fired. They said I didn't take direction well."

"Is that true?"

"Absolutely."

"Then it didn't have anything to do with the, uh, incident with Vivian?"

"No," I said. "Don't worry about it."

The restaurant shooting had been a small part of it, in fact. Internal Affairs had claimed I should have identified myself as an off-duty police officer and fired a warning shot. Or recognized a "hostage situation" and called for reinforcements. They called that Modern Police Procedure. It's hard on innocent bystanders, but, my, how neat the paperwork looks.

George groaned like a creaky cellar door. I followed his eyes to the tennis court.

Vivian had dropped her racquet and hoisted her tennis skirt above her waist. She stood flatfooted, with her legs spread. She shoved one hand down those white panties lady tennis players wear, and she scratched her crotch savagely. "Shit, shit, shit," she said in a small, shrill voice that carried well.

On the other side of the court, Mrs. Mollison stood with her hand over her face. Then she squared her shoulders, walked around the net and put her arm on Vivian's shoulders. They left the tennis court and walked slowly toward the house. Vivian let herself be led through a door at the far end of the patio.

When I looked at George, his eyes were closed, but not tightly enough to stop the tears.

Until then, I had no idea what rich, fulfilling lives the nouveau riche enjoyed.

George shook his head like a dog awakening and he blinked repeatedly.

"George," I said, "I don't know what you want from me. Am I supposed to ignore that? Or do you want to tell me about it?"

He croaked something unintelligible, coughed into a loose fist, and started again. "It's about Vivian," he said. "She was kidnapped last year."

"Awful quiet kidnapping."

"Yes. The press never found out."

"That's hard to figure," I said. "Are we talking about a we-got-your-kid, send-lots-of-money kidnapping or a leave-me-alone, I'm-an-adult squabble?"

"Well, maybe it wasn't a kidnapping in the classic sense."

"Okay, so what was it?"

"In a minute," he said. "I have the details inside." George smiled jerkily, briefly, and stood up. He pushed his chair back under the table. The legs screeched on the flagstones and he winced. "Be right back."

After George went into the house, the maid came out and offered me another drink. Her eyes were as beautiful as before; her smile made living and breathing seem worthwhile.

George was gone for several minutes. When he returned, he had a tooled leather attache case and a stiff-upper-lip, all-business approach. "Vivian," he said briskly, "was working on her Master's at SMU. In sociology. Her thesis was to be a study of hierarchy in modern tribes, specifically in motorcycle gangs."

"Wonderful," I said. "My favorite people."

George looked puzzled. "Motorcycle gangs? Or sociologists?"

"Neither, actually. Go on, don't mind me."

"Uh, yes, well, Vivian had somehow gained the confidence of one of the smaller gangs, according to her notes."

"According to her notes?"

"Yes," said George. "You see, once our living standard changed to, um, this—" He waved his hand vaguely at a million dollars of, *um, this.* "Vivian felt uncomfortable. At least, that's what she told us. She was away at school by then, and we seemed to hear less and less from her."

I thought about that "away at school" remark. Without standing up, I could have tossed a rock onto the SMU campus. Well, almost.

"Okay," I said. "She didn't keep you up-to-date on her school and social life. It happens. What does she say *now*?"

"Uh, this is difficult, Rafferty. Please let me tell it at my own pace."

"Go."

"As I said, she was studying a motorcycle gang. They planned an outing of some sort; a club ride and camping trip. Vivian phoned us three days before. She had been invited, she said, and she was quite excited about it. She thought it would give her new insights for her research."

"I'll bet."

"So she went away with the motorcycle gang," George said. "She didn't come back."

"Why not?"

"During the trip, they sold her."

CHAPTER TWO

"They sold her," George said again, before he blinked twice and popped the catches on his fancy attache case. He hid behind the raised lid and shuffled through papers.

I dug my pipe out of my hip pocket, packed it, and turned the top half-inch of tobacco into blue smoke. A stone ashtray the size of a wading pool materialized on the table and the shy brown maid ducked back into the house.

A big jet whistle-screamed overhead. The town planners thought they had stopped all that a dozen years ago, when they kicked the airlines out of Love Field. The dummies.

George sounded like he was building a nest in his fancy case.

"Okay," I said. "They sold her. Tell me the rest of it."

"Yes," he said behind the case. "To five men on motorcycles. She was missing for ten months." He surfaced, still blinking, avoiding my eyes. He carefully selected files from the case and stacked them in the center of the table. The stack was extremely neat. "Eventually, they abandoned her in a state park near Daingerfield," he said. "She was, uh, not well at the time."

A new voice said, "My husband finds this difficult to discuss, Mr. Rafferty. You'll have to forgive him." Mrs.

Mollison slipped into the chair next to George and put her left hand over his. With her free hand, she ground a cigarette butt into the big ashtray like she wanted to push it through the table.

"Hi," I said. "Been a long time."

She nodded. "Thank you for coming."

Marge Mollison was tall and slender and vaguely antiseptic in her tennis whites. Her blue eyes were clear, and her sharp white teeth were perfect, and her skin was smooth for a woman of her age.

Still, she was flawed. The problem wasn't her component parts; it was the way the package was assembled. Her face was oddly narrow. It had too many angles and not enough flesh. She had no hips. Her feet were surprisingly large. And she wore her hair very short, like a brown furry helmet. The hair style didn't suit her. Or then again, maybe it did.

"Vivian was worse than 'not well,' " Marge said calmly. "She was thirty pounds underweight, malnourished, and anemic. Her mind had been affected, probably by prolonged drug abuse. In addition, she had a raging case of gonorrhea and, we have since discovered, genital herpes."

"Well," I said, "we're finally getting to the point here. How is Vivian now?"

Marge shrugged. "Physically, much better. Mentally, it appears she may never recover from the drug effects. Doctor Rogerson, her psychologist, is not optimistic, at any rate. Apparently, those men kept her high continually."

"Does she act normal? Or does she just sit around and drool?"

George winced.

"Look," I said, "if you want dry medical watermelon talk, listen to her shrink. If you want maudlin sympathy, try the country club bar. You didn't ask me here for that sort of thing."

Marge Mollison nodded. She squeezed her husband's hand and said to me, "Vivian is lucid about a third of the time. Even then, she confuses dates and cannot remember if a specific event happened yesterday or five years ago. Her attention span is very short." Marge sighed. "As you saw, her approach to life is disgustingly basic. When we first got her back, she ate with her hands and had to be reminded to change clothes. Her personal habits were horrible. She would urinate wherever she happened to be, rather than walk to a bathroom. Fortunately, she is almost back to normal in that respect."

"This Rogerson quack," I said. "Does he think the mental and behavioral problems come from what those clowns did to her?"

"Yes, he does," said Marge. "George made a copy of his report. You may read it."

"I am easily bored by twelve syllable Latin derivatives. Tell me what you think it says."

She said, "Basically, Doctor Rogerson believes her self-esteem has been destroyed. Those men treated her as an object, a *thing*. After months of that treatment—while constantly drugged—Vivian has no feeling of self-worth. She considers herself valueless."

"Has she identified the men?"

George cleared his throat and gestured at the stack of files. "It's all in here," he said.

I puffed smoke at the sky and waited for them to ask. Rafferty's Rule Number Eight: The client has to say out loud what he wants me to do.

"I want you to find them, Rafferty," George said.

"Okay," I said.

"When you do," Marge said, "I want you to kill them."

"No. I don't do that kind of work."

"Rafferty," she said, "those men *used* Vivian. They infected her and they threw her away like a . . . like a used contraceptive. They stole her self-respect. They do not deserve to live."

"Probably not. Helluva shame I'm not in the vengeance business."

Marge folded her arms across her chest and glared at me. Somehow I managed to hold up under the pressure. I'm so tough it surprises me at times.

"What makes you think you can find them?" asked George. "The police—"

"The police won't do much about a missing adult. You probably found that out when you first reported her missing. And if they couldn't find her in ten months, they won't find the men who had her. Not if she's as lousy a witness as Marge says. And, when cops know they don't have a solid court case, they tend to lose interest."

Marge fished a pack of Virginia Slims and a gold lighter out of her tennis skirt. She fired up and said, "And you can do these things better than the police?"

"That's why I'm so all-fired effective, ma'am."

"You're not funny."

"Maybe not. But I'm good; the best you'll find. If you want this done, you need me."

"I want it done," she said, "and I want them dead, not out on bail because of some legal loophole. Dead!"

"Here's the best I can offer you," I said. "If I can't bring them in any other way, I'll leave the bodies on the doorstep so you can gloat over them. Those I don't have to kill—well, you have plenty of money. You can buy publicity and politicians. You can force the cops to take an active interest if I deliver the bikers on a platter."

George shook his head. "I don't remember you being so . . . so sour."

"Long time ago. I was young then. I thought the system worked." I knocked the ashes out of my pipe into the ashtray. Good ashtray, that one. Solid.

Marge took a deep angry drag on her Virginia Slim. George spread his hands vaguely. "How much money do you want?" he asked. "Two hundred dollars a day? Isn't that usual?"

"You watch *Magnum* and *The Rockford Files,* do you? Sorry, but this isn't a daily rate kind of job. Let's say three thousand apiece. That's fifteen for all five of them. Plus expenses. There might be some traveling involved."

Marge sniffed. "You don't look as if you've ever seen fifteen thousand dollars at one time."

"Hope springs eternal," I said. "Poor boy makes good.

Besides, there's Rafferty's Rule Number Five: If a client can afford it, he—or she—pays top dollar.''

George found a business card in his attache case, put it on top of the files, and pushed the stack toward me. "My attorney's card," he said. "He'll give you a check for whatever you need."

"Thanks," I said. "Now, Vivian doesn't sound like she can tell me much about those clowns, but I should talk to her."

"No, I'm afraid not," Marge said. "She doesn't relate to men very well."

"Violent?"

"No. That would be better," she said. "The problem is that Vivian was used as a sexual object for so long she now has a distorted view of relationships, however casual. She automatically offers herself to any man who approaches her."

George closed his eyes and turned his head away.

"I'm a big boy, Marge," I said. "I can be so honorable it hurts."

"It's not that," she said. "Meeting men puts Vivian back in her recovery. And it wouldn't help you to talk to her, Rafferty, believe me. Even George can't get anywhere with her. When he gave her a birthday present last month, she fondled him."

George lurched out of his chair and stumbled a dozen steps down his perfect lawn. He stood with his back to us and his head bowed.

Marge showed me out.

In the long circular driveway, my old Mustang leaned against the brick edging and quietly rusted in the sunlight. I wondered idly if the neighborhood Mercedes and Volvos would come around later to sniff the gravel like territorial dogs.

Marge fired up another cigarette while we stood on the front steps. She tilted her head and squinted through the smoke. "Why don't we say five thousand apiece," she said, "but only for the dead ones?"

"No, thanks. By the way, did you know certain Indian

tribes always gave their prisoners to the squaws? They thought the women were better at torture.''

''I didn't know that,'' she said, ''but it's a wonderful idea.''

CHAPTER THREE

I parked the Mustang in a lot on McKinney, locked Mollison's files in the trunk, then walked two blocks up and one over, to the only antique shop I liked.

Gardner's Antiques had fifty feet of sidewalk frontage, plate glass windows on each side of the door and tasteful gold lettering with elaborate serifs. All the items in the display windows had four-figure price tags.

A salesman spotted me three steps inside the front door and flounced over on an interception course. He had a purple silk shirt, no hips, and a supercilious look. "May I help you, sir?" he said. He didn't seem overwhelmed by the idea.

He caught me in front of a massive old sideboard. It was dark and heavy. It smelled of fresh polish. It had a maple top roughly the size of an aircraft carrier's flight deck. I thumped the glossy wood with my fist. The sideboard didn't even tremble. Purple Shirt smiled nervously.

"Yep," I said. "This might do."

"Oh?" he said tentatively. "It is a beautiful piece, isn't it? Early Victorian, of course, with a marvelous patina."

"If you say so. See, I need a new workbench for the garage. With storage space. I figure I could keep my tools in these drawers and put paint and stuff down below."

"Sir, this piece is—"

I slapped the sideboard again, harder this time. Purple Shirt jumped. "Do you think it's strong enough for me to bolt a vise on here?" I said. "And maybe put the bench grinder over there?" I whacked it again. My palm stung. "Hell, it'll do, I suppose. Will you take fifty bucks for it?"

His mouth twisted. "I get it now," he said. "You're Rafferty. She warned me about you."

"And you're new." I formed my right hand into a mock pistol, flipped my thumb down, and shot him between the eyes. "Gotcha! Where's Hilda?"

"In the back." He minced away.

It was always fun when Hilda hired new salesmen.

As Purple Shirt had promised, Hilda was in her office, plying the antique trade. In this case, the process consisted of frowning through half-moon reading glasses at an iridescent glass tumbler. Hilda compared the glass to glossy photos in a coffee-table-sized book. She didn't notice me in the doorway.

Hilda wore a severely tailored black suit; one of her hard-nosed business-lady outfits. Having some experience in the matter, I knew her underwear might be any color but would contrast sharply with the stark suit.

Hilda was like that; full of fascinating contradictions. Generally, she was calm and self-assured, as laid-back as a sleepy cat. Even then you could sense her latent energy.

Her driver's license said late thirties; her pale clear skin hinted at twenty-two.

Hilda's eyes were dark; coal-black at first glance. Up close—breath-mingling close—there were tiny flecks of color visible. I could never pin down exactly what those colors were, but they were there.

Hilda had a mop of errant dark hair that looked uncombed. It had been combed—she was enough of a lady to work at it—but she managed to do without those gawdawful plastic curlers that populate the supermarkets.

People who knew us both said I was lucky to be involved with Hilda. They were right.

She frowned again, inverted the glass tumbler, and peered at the bottom of it.

"McDonald's, circa 1978," I said. "Somebody put it in the dishwasher and the decals came off."

"Peasant," she said. "What would you know?" She flipped the big book shut, carefully put the glass on a table near her desk, and stood up to be kissed.

We made a proper job of it. When we finally broke, she grinned up at me. "You missed me," she said.

"You bet, gorgeous. How was your trip?"

"Not bad," she said. "I got a nice Victorian blanket chest in the furniture lot. And some fair glassware, including that tumbler. I'm sure it's Tiffany, even though he didn't sign it."

"Damned inconsiderate of old Louis Comfort."

"Well, well. You're learning."

"I know a broad who's in the business. She teaches me things."

"I see. Some old harridan, I suppose."

"No. She's not a bad looker, now that I think about it. Black, black hair that fluffs out around her face. Great legs, too, and a cute little mole to the left of—"

"Rafferty, " Hilda said sternly, "if you're trying to turn me on, you're out of luck. I cannot get away this afternoon. Honestly. Tonight, well, if you play your cards right . . ."

"You won't be able to miss me. I'll be under a cold shower. Hey, babe, I'm working, too, for a change. I'll be busy today myself."

"Are you walking around with that jewelry salesman again or is this something interesting?"

"Sad is a better word than interesting, I think. I'll tell you about it tonight."

"Okay," said Hilda. She squeezed my hand. "I missed you, Ugly. It seemed like longer than five days."

"Yes," I said. "It certainly did."

T. L. Dermott had a plush office near the top of Bryan Tower. He also had a florid, unhealthy complexion and a protective attitude about the Mollisons.

"Mr. Rafferty," he said solemnly, "I must tell you I

advised George and Margaret not to pursue such an ill-advised adventure.''

"Is that so?''

"Yes," he went on, "it is. Unfortunately, they have decided not to heed that advice.''

"Wow, that's good news. I was terribly nervous for a minute there.''

Dermott pursed his thick lips. "Mr. Rafferty, understand me. I like to think I am a Mollison family friend as well as their attorney. They have been brutalized by Vivian's experience. I simply do not believe prolonging that horror will help them.''

I shrugged. "You may be right. Since your objection is philosophical, I assume you aren't going to haggle about the money, then?''

"Of course not. It's their money. Besides, a few dollars for your expenses will hardly be missed.''

"Thanks for the vote of confidence," I said. "So where did Mollison make all his dough, anyway? Way back when, he wasn't well heeled.''

Dermott nodded. "True. George was—is—an electronics engineer, you know. Actually, that understates the case. The man is technically brilliant. He developed a super-efficient microchip.'' Dermott shrugged dismissively. "Of course, new technology crops up fairly often these days. There is no shortage of gifted designers. But George went a step further. He developed a manufacturing process to produce his unique microchip. And—most important of all—that process was patentable. Today, seventy-four percent of all microprocessor manufacturers use the Mollison process.''

"I read somewhere the bottom is falling out of the small computer market. Again.''

"All markets fluctuate, Mr. Rafferty. If one or two firms go out of business, well, so what? They will be replaced by others who need the Mollison process. Or existing firms will absorb their share of the marketplace. Meanwhile, the Mollisons' cash flow from royalty income is substantial.''

"I noticed.''

"Hmm? Oh, their home. I arranged a rather attractive short-term mortgage on that property. We shoved most of the interest into the first year. Nice income off-set while we structured the rest of the portfolio."

I said, "You're the financial planning whiz kid, I assume."

Dermott smiled modestly. "I deserve some of the credit, yes. The Mollisons were rather unsophisticated, financially, but George had good instincts. He knew when to rely on expert help. I assembled a very talented group of tax people and investment advisers. We then devised a program to continually roll the royalty income over into investments. Aside from the Highland Park home, the first acquisitions were evenly divided between long-range security and income-producing items; although lately, I have— Well, it's no concern of yours, is it?"

"No," I said. "Poor old George. Must be a rough way to live."

Dermott said gently, "When you put Vivian's condition into the equation, it is, in fact, a strange existence for them. They have a lovely home, a magnificent income, and an abundance of leisure time. Too much leisure time, really. George doesn't have anything to take his mind off the problem."

"Ouch. Point taken. Sorry."

"No matter. Now, what can I do for you, Mr. Rafferty, besides tell tales out of school?"

"I need expense money. Say, two thousand for starters."

Dermott's eyebrows went up, but he buzzed Miss Somebody on the intercom and told her to make out a check. Then he turned back to me and said, "I have no experience in these matters, but I assume the motorcycle gang will violently oppose you in this half-baked, um, quest."

"I'm a pretty violent guy myself, Counselor."

"Oh, really?"

I smiled at him blandly. "It may not show right now. On the way over here, I kicked a couple of dogs and crippled a meter maid. I'll be fairly mellow until the high wears off."

Dermott rolled his eyes. We waited silently for Miss Whoosis to bring the check.

Dermott's check was written on a bank on Commerce Street, so I strolled over to cash it. The bank was one of those modern, streamlined places. Every surface was light and shiny. The air-conditioning was set ten degrees too low. The place had the ambience of a public urinal.

The cash made a healthy stack, though, and it felt good to tuck crisp new hundreds in my wallet. Having Mollison's money was one thing, of course. Earning it was another.

I checked in with my answering service. There were no calls. Neither the girl on duty nor I were surprised. It didn't matter. I was working again, Hilda was back, and summertime in downtown Dallas was great for girl-watching.

I got the car out of hock and headed north on Central Expressway, thinking about bikers and how to find them. It didn't seem likely I'd run them down through the usual public records.

I found one sooner than I expected, when an ugly black motorcycle rumbled past me on the Lemmon Avenue overpass. The guy riding it looked like a cross between a wino and Attila the Hun. He wore jeans and a black T-shirt, and a vest made by ripping the sleeves off a denim jacket. There were ornate patches on the back of the denim vest, but I couldn't read them because a fat, flat-faced woman sat behind the rider. Both bikers' clothes were as dirty as the motorcycle was clean.

The bike took the Mockingbird Lane exit a hundred yards before I did, and we both stopped at a red light two blocks later.

It occurred to me that I could have the names and photographs of the five bikers who bought Vivian Mollison and I would still have trouble picking them out in a crowd. This turkey, for example, was faceless behind a bushy blond beard and mirror sunglasses. He had a cloth headband and a beer gut. And he was twenty years too old to be playing with motorcycles.

I rolled my window down. The exhaust note of the bike drowned out a truck on the cross street. The biker swiveled his head toward me and blipped the bike's throttle. The motor revved, then idled down with a curious slapping sound.

Roar. Slap-slap-slap. Roar. Roar. Slap-slap-slap.

Big goddamned deal.

I smiled at him. "How ya doing, pal?" I said to the noise. "Bought any good blondes lately?"

The light changed and the bike jumped away. As it cut into my lane, the fat woman turned around and flipped me the finger.

She must have missed the part about making a new friend each and every day.

CHAPTER FOUR

I went home and waded through the files Mollison had given me. Some of the material was interesting; some of it was garbage, especially a long-winded report by the shrink named Rogerson. He spent six pages bragging about how he toilet-trained Vivian. To me, he seemed overly interested in the details.

There was also a medical report from a real doctor. It was dry and dusty and I didn't understand much of the medical jargon, but there seemed no doubt that Vivian had been in bad shape when the bikers dumped her.

There was a Xerox of a field report by the Morris County deputy sheriff who had found Vivian. There was a letter from the Grayson County sheriff to Mollison. It admitted he had not yet found the "perpetrators," but promised continued effort.

There was a handwritten note by Mollison that summarized a meeting with the Dallas cops. The tone of the note was suspicious, but there were two intriguing items in it: the leader of the Dallas bikers was now dead and Ed Durkee had worked the case.

There was also a ten-page report by AllTex Investigations. The report was neatly assembled in a fake leather binder and held together by those white plastic curlicues. It had been typed on an expensive carbon-ribbon machine. Offhand, I guessed the report had cost the Mollisons at least five hundred bucks a page and all it did was summarize the police and medical files.

I knew about AllTex. An ex-FBI guy ran it. They were pure hell on paperwork and customer relations, but they hated to get their hands dirty.

I wondered who else George had tried before he came to me.

I had planned to distill the pile of official information myself, but the hotshots with their two-thousand-dollar typewriter had already done that. So, I put my pad away, made coffee, ignited the pipe, and settled back with the AllTex contribution to the Book-of-the-Month Club.

Vivian had contacted the Dallas DeathStars, a local motorcycle gang. She traveled with them on a weekend ride to Lake Texoma, a big Corps of Engineers waterway seventy miles north of Dallas on the Oklahoma border. On Monday, the bikers returned to Dallas. Without Vivian.

The DeathStars leader, a local thug named Guts Holman, was suspected of handing her over to a small group of bikers the DeathStars had met during the weekend. Holman didn't have any comment about that claim, mostly because he was killed four days later when his Harley-Davidson came out second best in an argument with a loaded cement truck.

Ten months after that, the Morris County deputy found Vivian near Daingerfield.

When Vivian had not returned, the Mollisons reported her missing. The various police organizations went to work on it, but they had barely found their carbon paper when Holman went to the big motorcycle shop in the sky. The other DeathStars conveniently developed collective amnesia.

The case drifted off into that "we're working on it, but don't ask us how" limbo found in any busy cop shop. Much later, when Vivian had been found, she had not contributed enough information to induce official enthusiasm.

All the police letters and reports agreed on one thing: there was no sign of the five men who supposedly bought Vivian. And nobody even knew who they were.

Putting together Vivian's incoherent ramblings and the usual collection of blind hopes and wild guesses, it boiled down to this. The men Marge Mollison wanted to see bleeding on her lawn were called Smokey Joe, Bad Bill, Stomper, Frog, and Turk. One of them—no one knew which—probably had the name Becker on his birth certificate. Another possible last name was Conover, but there was a little town by that name near Daingerfield, so flip a coin on that one.

By the time I finished digesting the report, it was almost six o'clock. I left a note for Hilda and went out for food. Twenty minutes later, I came back with two pounds of ribs and the extras. Hilda's red BMW was parked in front of the house.

She was inside, sipping a tall drink and leafing through the medical report from the Mollison files. "Hi, sweetheart," she said. "I wondered if you'd gotten a better offer."

"Never happen. Ribs okay for supper?"

"Yumm." Hilda frowned and waved the report. "Hey, what is this?"

"Part of the job I got today." I put the ribs in the oven to stay warm. "You aren't hungry yet, are you?"

Hilda smiled. She had changed clothes. Now she wore a white jumpsuit with zippers in every possible location. I tried one at random. It turned out to be a pocket.

"Cold," she said. "Very cold. Try again."

The next zipper released a pleat built into the side. The jumpsuit billowed loosely. "Whoops," I said. "Now no one can tell you're not wearing underwear."

"I can't understand it," Hilda said. "The man claims he missed me, but he can't find one lousy little zipper."

As it turned out, all the zippers on the front were wrong.

There was a long one down the back, however, that did the job very nicely.

"Yes," said Hilda as she stepped out of the jumpsuit, "I think we should let the ribs age for an hour or so."

CHAPTER FIVE

I took the ribs out of the oven and put a half dozen on each of our plates.

Hilda said, "Don't you want to get dressed first?"

"No. Ribs should be eaten while naked. Rafferty's Rule Eighteen."

We ate at the kitchen counter, sitting on bar stools, gnawing ribs, dirtying paper napkins by the dozen, and loving it.

Despite Rule Eighteen, Hilda wore a thin robe. It was bright yellow, which made a nice contrast to her dark hair. She had a soft after-bed look in her eyes and a smear of barbecue sauce on her left cheek.

"You know," I said, "despite your advanced age, you are one good-looking broad."

"You really know how to treat a lady, don't you, Ugly? In case you've forgotten, you're two years older than I am."

"Ah, but that's only on the outside. Down deep, I'm nineteen. Maybe twenty on a bad day."

"Hmph," snorted Hilda. She tapped her temple. "In here, you're about five hundred. Sir Rafferty of Dallas Castle. Dragons slain while you wait."

"If you're going to start that knight crap again, I'll eat the last of the cole slaw."

"What else is new?" she said, "I'm full, anyway. Tell me what you did while I was away."

"Nothing much. The Cowboys cheerleaders dropped by. Nice girls. It took me three days to get around to all of them."

"Three days?" Hilda said. "You must be getting old."

"It wasn't my fault. They kept running cheers. Gimme an 'R', gimme an 'A'—"

"Seriously," she said. "What about this new job you mentioned?"

I told her about Vivian Mollison and the bikers.

Hilda shivered. "Ugh! They ought to hang people like that. Slowly. In public."

"What the hell is this?" I said. "First, Marge Mollison offers me a bonus for the bodies. I think she plans to cut off their ears or something. Now you want to sell tickets for a lynch mob. Did Margaret Thatcher take over the feminist movement when I wasn't looking?"

"You're not going to kill them? Assuming you catch them, I mean."

"Don't know. It will be up to them, probably. It usually is."

"Yes, I know, dear," Hilda said patiently. "But *bikers*, after all. They won't come in peacefully, will they?"

"No," I said, "probably not."

"So you may have to kill one or more of them. Again, assuming you can find them."

"Hil, babe, will you stop this 'assuming you can find them' business? I'll find them. I think."

"Sorry," she said. "I just don't see how—Oh, forget it. I must have the postcoital megrims. You want coffee?"

"Rafferty's Rule Twenty-eight: Hot coffee and nudity don't mix. If you spill, it hurts. I'll have another beer."

"Aha! Got you this time," said Hilda, grinning. "Two months ago, you told me Rule Twenty-eight was something about demanding recent blood tests from women who didn't gasp when you got undressed."

"No, you've got that all wrong. Hell, you didn't gasp the first time."

"Whoops! Slipped up in the maidenly vapors department, did I?"

"I didn't say anything because I figured, what the hell, you might teach me some new tricks."

"Get your butt back into that bedroom, Ugly. I'll show you tricks."

"Terrific. There's a fresh can of Redi-Whip around here somewhere, too."

"Redi-Whip? And no chopped nuts? Jeez, you are a cheap bastard."

CHAPTER SIX

The next morning, Hilda left to change at her place before meeting one of her Turtle Creek antique customers. She was excited about unloading a Georgian gilt moustache cup. Or some such.

I drove downtown to the cop shop. Professional courtesy. Besides, I wanted help.

Ed Durkee looked less like a police lieutenant than anyone else you could imagine. He was a shambling bear of a man with a face like a basset hound. He wore a brown suit. Always. Ed must have had a closetful of those brown suits, each one rumpled and poorly tailored. The only way you could tell Ed ever changed clothes was that some of his brown suits were old enough to have cuffs.

"Ed," I said, "you won't make it in this line of work unless you have the right clothes. Buy yourself a Stetson, a nice pair of lizard-skin boots, maybe a string tie. You're a Texas cop, pal. You can't dress like a third-rate soap salesman and expect to make captain."

Durkee scrawled his signature on a file, tossed it on top of a ragged stack in his out basket, and frumped. "Look who's talking," he said. "Man doesn't even own a suit."

31

"Sure I do. It's not brown, though. It's sort of a muted gray. Very classy."

"Yeah?" he said. "And when did you last wear it?"

"In 1975, I think. Maybe '76."

Ed snorted and signed another file. "What do you want, Rafferty? I'm busy."

"Vivian Mollison. Her father got tired of waiting for you guys to get hot. He sought professional help, as it were."

Durkee wheezed, "You? Oh, sure, you blew away that junkie when the kid was little. And caught a reprimand, too, as I remember."

"So? Some people need blowing away."

"Ain't it the truth? Wait a minute, I'll get Ricco in here. We might be able to give you something."

Ed and I were drinking bitter coffee from dimestore mugs when Sergeant Ricco sauntered in. Ricco, as usual, affected a hippy-dippy walk. It made him look like his underwear was too tight.

"There, Ed," I said, gesturing at Ricco, "there's a man who knows how to dress."

Ricco was short, skinny, and overly neat. His clothes were cheap-sharp, but they hadn't been wrinkled since 1947. Trouble was, Ricco thought he was loaded with street smarts and he worked too hard at maintaining the image. He had never learned to hide the rat-cunning in his face.

Ricco wasn't a bad cop, actually. His appearance was the problem. He always seemed ready to offer you a hot deal on a repainted Corvette or a machine gun or his virgin sister. It was hard to take him seriously.

Ed told Ricco what I wanted. "So let's give him what we have," Ed said. "I can't allocate manpower for a wild goose chase after those no-name bikers, but I wouldn't mind seeing *somebody* look around, even if it's only Rafferty."

"That's it, Ed," I said. "You are definitely out of the will."

"You're doing the right thing," said Ricco. "He don't deserve to inherit. So, anyway, how much do you know?"

"Vivian Mollison went away with a crowd of low-lifes on bikes. She didn't come back. Her folks claim the bikers sold her. Tell me about this clown Holman."

"Best thing about that asshole is he's dead," said Ricco. "Though he may not know it yet. Dumb son-of-a-bitch had an IQ about twelve."

"You believe this story about Holman selling Vivian to another group of bikers?"

"Oh, yeah," said Ricco. "It fits. Holman was that speed. He got busted half a dozen times in Houston, all strong back, weak mind stuff. Assault, CCW, a couple of nickel-and-dime dope busts."

"That's a far cry from selling lady sociologists at a swap meet."

"Naw, not really. We had Holman fitted for a beef like that before this Mollison thing. That time, he recruited some jailbait from the projects. When he got tired of the bitch, he passed her around to those mouth-breathers in his gang. Well, she thought it had been true love or some fucking thing, so she didn't like that, see? She told her folks and they all trooped in here one day. The kid was ready to testify Holman was getting paid for her." Ricco shook his head. "Thought we had the prick that time."

"What happened?"

"You figure it out. The slut's father suddenly came down with a broken arm, see, and his face looked like a pizza. He fell down the stairs, he says. And chicky-poo lost her memory. Can't remember nothing, she says. Holman who? Oh, and by the way, she says, we're moving to San Antonio. Daddy heard about this great job down there lugging garbage cans." Ricco shrugged. "No witness, no case. But it was close enough to the Mollison deal for me. He sold her."

"Where did you hear about the sale part of it?" I asked. "From Vivian?"

"No way," said Ricco. "The Mollison girl's been a fucking zombie ever since she got loose."

Ed said, "We picked it up from an informant. Holman

bragged about sucking in a woman shrink, then off-loading her to five Oklahoma bikers for four hundred bucks."

"How reliable is your snitch? I haven't heard the part about Oklahoma until now."

Ricco shrugged. Ed said, "How reliable is any snitch? Maybe seven on a scale of ten."

"So, you got nothing at all out of Holman?"

"Come on! If he had admitted anything, we wouldn't have let him go get killed. The fact is, our timing was lousy. We never talked to Holman about it. The way it happened, while the snitch was telling Ricco about Holman, the quacks at Parkland were pulling a sheet up over his face."

"How far did you get with Holman's biker buddies?"

"Nowhere," said Durkee. "Didn't matter whether Guts Holman was dead or alive, they wouldn't talk. We did get a tip last week, though. I don't think it's much—not enough to put my people on it—but you can have it."

"Oh, joys of joys," I said. "I'll try to do a good job, Ed, and make you real proud of me."

"Jesus Christ, Rafferty. If you ask me, they got rid of you just in time. Go on, Ricco, tell him."

Ricco leaned in close to tell me his big secret. He had eaten sausage for breakfast. You can't fool a sharp investigator like me.

"Here's the deal," Ricco said. "One of the DeathStars split up with his old lady. Way I hear it, she was never really into that grubby Levis and vroom-vroom shit, anyway. And the word is, she's been bad-mouthing the bikers since she walked out on hubby. You might get something out of her."

"That's it?"

"Whatta you want?" protested Ricco. "I wouldn't give you that much, except Ed won't let me take time to work it myself."

"We've been all through that, Ricco," Ed said. "I'm supposed to get my butt chewed so you can go gawk at the strippers?"

Ricco grinned wickedly. "See, this ginch works at one

of them beer joint topless places on Industrial,'' he said. "Name's Fran Zifretti. Well, maybe not Zifretti, 'cause she might not be using her old man's name now, but Fran, anyway.''

"Okay, thanks,'' I said. "I see why you're not willing to use your overtime budget on it, Ed. Now, how about a little more? Like the file on the DeathStars, maybe?''

Ed looked sad and sour. Normal, in other words.

"Ricco,'' he said, "give Rafferty a list of the gang members. If he doesn't get his teeth kicked out, he might get somebody to talk about the Mollison girl.''

"Thanks, Ed. And you may rest assured I will carefully remind them about *Miranda* and *Escobedo* and all that. I wouldn't want to violate their civil rights.''

"Yeah,'' Durkee yawned, "I'll bet. What the hell, you can get away with stomping some toad for information. We can't. Good luck.''

Ricco went away to dredge up the list for me. I smoked a pipe and watched Ed work through his paper mountain. Rafferty's Rule for Modern Police Work: No arrest is permissible until the weight of the paperwork equals the weight of the suspect.

When Ricco came back twenty minutes later, I had finished my pipe and Ed had signed thirty-seven files.

I figured we were just about even on useful work completed.

CHAPTER SEVEN

There must be five hundred bars in Texas named the Dew Drop Inn. Mostly, they aren't the sort of place to take your elderly mother when she comes to visit. And the Dew Drop Inn where Fran Zifretti worked was definitely not on the maternal tourist list.

That afternoon, a nasal voice had answered the phone and told me Fran wouldn't come in until six. I gave it a couple of hours extra and arrived a little after eight.

The exterior decor was 1950s Public Toilet: white concrete block with a flat roof and a scabrous parking lot on all four sides. It was a block off Industrial Boulevard, between a tire retreading plant and a place that manufactured sheet metal ductwork.

The Dew Drop Inn didn't look like a meeting place for The Beautiful People.

I parked my Mustang on the outside edge of the parking lot, where it couldn't be blocked in. I locked my wallet in the glove compartment, folded a twenty and a fifty into small squares, and tucked them deep in separate pockets.

I had dressed in old jeans, boots, a Cowboys T-shirt, and a nylon windbreaker. The evening was too warm for the windbreaker, but it hid the shoulder-holstered .38 nicely. And I had my old Ithaca twelve-gauge pump under a blanket on the back seat.

It was that kind of a Dew Drop Inn.

The inside of the place was nearly as depressing as the outside. There was one large rectangular room with booths set against the walls. The bar formed a square, off-set toward the entrance. Inside the bar square, there was a head-high stage, roughly ten feet on a side, with baby spots around the edge.

Between the stage and the bar, there were two bartenders listlessly cleaning glasses. I bet myself they never bothered to turn around and look up at the girls.

At the other end of the room, there were two pool tables, four round tables with chairs, and a jukebox playing mournful country music. And a corridor going away. Toilets and an office, probably.

The lighting was halfway between cocktail-bar dim and see-the-grime bright. There was a thin blue pall of cigarette smoke and a sour smell in the room.

I looked at the mess behind the bar and decided against draft beer. I ordered a bottle of Bud instead and leaned against the bar, wondering which of the girls was Fran Zifretti. There were four of them, sitting in booths, hustling drinks, wearing only bikini bottoms, and pushing their chests at the suckers.

The bartender brought me my change. Not enough change for one lousy beer, but it was Mollison's expense money. What was I, the Better Business Bureau?

I shoved a buck back at the bartender and said, "Where's Fran?"

He made the bill disappear before my very eyes and jerked his head at the stage above and behind him. "She's on next. Five minutes."

Halfway through the beer, a bouncy redhead trotted out of the back corridor, ducked under the bar service hatch and up steep steps to the stage. A bartender pushed buttons and snapped switches. The baby spots came on and the jukebox died in mid-whine. A cassette tape player hiccuped, then kicked in at high volume with a thumping disco beat.

Ricco was wrong. Fran Zifretti hadn't climbed onto the stage to take off her clothes. She was already stripped down to standard uniform for the Dew Drop: bikini bottoms and boobs. Standard dance: stylized jiggling and arm-waving. There's no business like show business, et cetera.

Had to give her credit, though. She tried. She mugged her way through quick eager smiles and outrageous winks. Her amateur bumps and grinds were enthusiastic. And half a beat off the rhythm.

Despite her efforts, the crowd was unmoved. Two leathery men on my side of the bar were lost in an argument about which was better, Mack or Peterbilt. The bartenders never turned around—I won my personal bet—and, except for a toothless old-timer in a booth, I was Fran's only audience.

I grinned at her, using my disarming smile. Hilda claimed it was more oafish than disarming, but I kept practicing. Everyone needs a hobby.

When I caught Fran's eye, I pointed at her, then at myself, then at my drink. She nodded. With that out of the way, I sipped my beer and watched her dance.

Fran Zifretti was twenty-fiveish, with a face that was plain, edging toward cute. She had a dusting of freckles that went with her red hair and she had a tan that didn't. Ah, well, not every redhead can have milky skin and a lilting Irish brogue.

Fran had good legs, a nice rump, and, overall, she would have had a terrific figure if her plastic surgeon hadn't ripped her off. Some doctor had a lot to answer for. Fran Zifretti's chest looked like someone had sliced a soccer ball in half and shoved the two domes under her skin.

Poor Fran. She bobbed and weaved, disco-hopped, and jounced. Her curly hair moved, her arms moved, the flesh on her thighs moved—hell, everything moved except her breasts. Those phony boobs just sat there like lumps of concrete. Okay, maybe they moved a little bit, but it didn't look right. The effect was similar to a man jogging while wearing a chest protector.

I wondered if it hurt and felt relieved for her when the music finally stopped and she climbed down from the stage.

She came straight toward me, smiling amiably as if we

were casual acquaintances meeting by chance in a super-market. No sultry looks, no posturing to emphasize her near-nudity, no extra hip swing. Fran Zifretti would never make it as a B-girl.

"Hi," she said, "how you doing?"

"Great," I said. "Sure did like your dance." I practiced my disarming smile again. Fran didn't wince. Maybe I was improving.

A bartender appeared as if by magic. "Buy the lady a drink?"

"Why not? Two more beers, my good man."

"The lady prefers champagne."

Fran looked around the grubby room and ignored our street theater performance.

"Tell you what, pal," I said to the bartender. "You ask the sommelier to bring the wine list. In the meantime, we'll have two beers."

The bartender frowned at Fran. She chimed in with, "How about a Manhattan? I love Manhattans."

"Okay," I said. "Another Bud and a Manhattan for the lady."

The bartender started to push the champagne again, but she cut him off. "A Manhattan, Chuck. That'll be fine."

Chuck the bartender brought a glass of iced tea disguised as a Manhattan, a second beer, and a quarter change for a ten. I didn't let him keep the quarter. He didn't seem surprised.

We took our drinks to a booth. Fran sipped her tea and smiled automatically. "Hey, I haven't seen you in here before."

"No," I said. "Look, Fran, I don't want to go through a big song-and-dance here. For one thing, I'll get angry if I have to buy a champagne bottle full of Seven-Up and for another, I want to be up-front with you. I want to talk about the DeathStars."

She had looked puzzled when I started talking. Now she looked disgusted. "Jesus," she said. "Those creeps. Who are you?"

"My name is Rafferty. I'm a friend of Vivian Mollison.

Tell me about the time Guts Holman sold her to the out-of-town bikers.''

"Oh, shit! Hey, I had nothing to do with that—"

"It's okay, Fran. That's what I hear, too," I said. "There's no trouble in this for you. Or the other Death-Stars, unless Holman had help."

"No," she said. "It was only Guts, I'm pretty sure. When he bragged about it later, some of the guys were really surprised, you know?"

"Okay, then. Tell me about Holman. He was the stud duck of the DeathStars, right?"

"Right. But . . ."

The Dew Drop Inn had begun to fill up. A pair of ropy-looking cowboy types started a pool game in the back. It looked noisy, though you couldn't be sure. A tall black girl was doing her version of a dance on the stage and her music was loud and bassy.

A fat greasy guy in dark jeans and a stained T-shirt leaned against the bar and sucked on a beer bottle. He had a black headband and a straggly beard. It was entirely possible he got his hardjutting belly from the same silicon-stuffer who did Fran's chest.

"Look," Fran said, "I gave up that biker bullshit when I dumped Tony. I'm out of it. I don't think I should talk about it." She frowned. "Besides, how do I know you're not a cop?"

"Beats the hell out of me, Fran. Do I look like a cop?"

"Nooo, not quite," she said. "You seem more . . . interested."

"You got it. I'm interested. I'm being paid to be interested, of course, but it's the sort of thing I might do as a hobby, anyway. Rafferty's Rule Twelve: Selling people is antisocial."

"So what are you, a private detective?"

"Investigator," I said automatically.

"What's the difference?"

"None, really. Except that cops don't like it if you call yourself a detective. They think it sounds too official. And people don't like to talk to 'detectives,' for the same reason. Investigator, on the other hand, sounds like insurance or credit ratings. Wimpy stuff like that.'' I gave her another disarming smile.

"Did you hurt your mouth or something?"

"Forget it," I said.

One of the other girls drifted over to our booth and we did Scene Two of *Buy The Lady A Drink*. I had to crack the fifty to pay for that round.

"Fran, this goddamn place is gonna break me while we swap pleasantries. I've told you the way this thing is going down. You, hubby Tony, and the other DeathStars can play big bad bikers all you want. Believe me, I don't care. Holman seems to be the only one who did the dirty on Vivian. And he gets a free ride because he's dead. All I want are the five clowns you met at Lake Texoma. That's all.''

She shook her head doubtfully. "I bet you don't find them."

"I'll find them, Fran. It's what I do. And, despite my shy, unassuming manner, I'm pretty good at what I do.''

"You say," she smiled, with a hint of a sneer. Then the sneer and the smile dropped away to a lifeless mask. She lowered her face and stared at the table.

"Hey, Clyde, how's it going? You having a good time slobbering over Frannie's tits?''

The jerk with the beard and belly stood near the booth. He tilted his beer bottle up to drain it while he kept his eyes on me. Implied threat. Tough guy. Big deal.

"Hey, Frannie," he said, "don'tcha say hello no more?''

"Hello, Goose," she said in a monotone.

At first, I had pegged Goose for thirtyish, but now, up close, I thought he was closer to my age. Or maybe not. Perhaps he looked older because of the dirt in the wrinkles around his eyes. Whatever.

No matter how old he was, he was a classic case of arrested development. He wore a gold earring and a replica Nazi ring with a skull. He used a length of chain for a belt.

His arms were tattooed. The general theme was eagles, with a smattering of toilet graffiti.

Goose said, "Clyde, man, your time is up. Give somebody else a chance to score with old Frannie Rottencrotch, hey?"

"He's right, mister," Fran said. "I better go now." She slid out of the booth. "Thanks for the drinks."

Goose laughed at me and followed Fran to the bar. They argued briefly, then Fran stalked away. One of the truck drivers stroked her backside, but she kept walking and disappeared down the back corridor.

She came back after twenty minutes or so, did another jerky, painful-looking dance, then sat at a table with two slumming salesmen and another house girl.

Goose stayed at the bar, swilling beer and playing hairy majordomo.

The black girl came to my booth and we tried Scene Three of the booze burlesque. I messed up my lines and she left before the curtain.

Five minutes later, a blonde with no breasts—but enormous nipples—came to bat, presumably to determine whether my problem was racial prejudice or diminished libido. Bartender Chuck made a personal appearance with a bottle of champagne that time. He started his pitch, then looked at my face and stopped in midsentence. He took the blonde with him when he left. At the bar, Goose guffawed.

I went to the salesmen's table and tried to take Fran aside long enough to get her phone number or address, but Goose moved in too quickly. I became less and less tolerant of my fellow man.

Chuck the bartender, after a hard look from Goose, decided he didn't know anything for twenty dollars and he declined to advance into the semifinals.

Goose had become a significant pain in the ass.

I found a pay phone in a corner and called Hilda at her place.

"It's late, Rafferty," she said. "Are you all right?"

"Oh, sure," I said. "I am frivolously disporting with

the jet-setters. They keep trying to sell me bottles of vintage champagne."

"What vintage?"

"June, I think. Or maybe July. Hil, babe, I just want to talk to you for a minute."

"Are you sure you're all right?"

"Yeah. A tad frustrated. I'm playing footsie with a prime, number-one cretin who's ripe for maiming, but I have to be careful how I do it. There's a frightened lady here who can tell me things I need to know."

Hilda said, "It always reassures me when you bring your little troubles home instead of taking them to strangers. It makes me feel so needed."

"Okay, okay. You going to be up for a while yet?"

"After this call, yes, I expect so."

"I might drop by."

"Bring hamburgers or something. I'm hungry."

"Will do. Bye, love."

"Rafferty," Hilda said. "you're weird."

"But lovable. Don't forget how lovable I am."

"There is that. See you later."

I hung up, walked over to where Fran sat with the salesmen, and handed her a business card. "Here. Phone me in the morning."

"But—" She looked sideways at Goose stomping our way.

"It's all right. Goose and I are about to settle this minor contretemps."

Goose arrived. "Gimme that," he said to Fran.

"Later, Goose," I said. "First, let's go outside, so I can kick the shit out of you."

Goose grinned. Two of his teeth were missing. Those remaining were muddy brown. "Now that's my man!" he said. "Let's do it."

I told Fran not to lose my card. "I'm expecting that call."

She slipped the card into her bikini pants.

"Lucky card," muttered one of the salesmen.

"Okay, Goose," I said. "Let's get it over with."

Outside, in the parking lot, he spun around and shuffled toward me with his arms held wide. That made sense. With his build, he was a good bet to be a bear-hugger.

"Wait one," I said. "Neither of us wants to get Fran fired. Let's go down the street a little way."

He straightened up and grunted. "You ain't getting out of this, chicken shit. Follow me." Goose swaggered to a black Harley parked near the front door. He took a black denim vest from the bike's handlebars and shrugged into it. On the back of the vest was a stylized skull on a starry background. Separate, curved patches above and below the skull said DEATHSTARS and DALLAS.

Which was about what I had guessed. Maybe I should offer a correspondence course. Famous Detective School.

Goose swung a thick leg over the bike and jabbed a finger at me. "Don't try to run, Clyde. You try to get away, I might decide to hurt you real bad." He snarled in case I wasn't sufficiently impressed, kicked his Harley in the guts, and blue-smoked the night air.

I walked to the Mustang, unlocked it, got in, started up, and waved him ahead. He made the first fifty feet with the front wheel in the air, then slowed to make sure I was following him. I took the shotgun off the back seat and laid it across my lap.

We convoyed through the quiet industrial district. Goose squirted ahead, then dropped back to wait for me. He made a series of rights and lefts, turned into a cul-de-sac ringed by electronics firms and stopped his motorcycle.

I ran down the Harley-Davidson. Goose jumped clear at the last minute. The bike made a satisfying clatter as the Mustang bounced over it. Metal screeched like a hurt animal. Something under the car tangled with the motorcycle for a moment, and I had to gun it hard in reverse to jerk free.

Tired old cars like the Mustang are so handy for that sort of thing.

"You cocksuckerrr!" Goose screamed as I got out of the car. I showed him my shotgun and he quieted down a bit.

"Hey, Clyde," he said, "we had us a fair fight set up here."

"Bullshit, Goose. I bet you haven't fought fair for twenty years. Come to think of it, neither have I." I tossed a load of shot into the motor and gas tank of the Harley. As the echo off the buildings faded, I jacked another shell into the chamber. *Scrick, scrack.* Nice counterpoint.

"What the fuck is the matter with you, man?" Goose said. "You crazy?"

"Pass the word to the turkeys you run with. I'm after the bikers who bought Vivian Mollison. Not you guys. But you stay out of my way when I'm trying to talk to Fran Zifretti or anyone else."

"You bastard," he said, pointing at his Harley. "You're not after me, but you did that to my *bike*?"

The Harley looked like it had fallen off a building. The frame was bent. Both wheels were mangled. There were bright pellet smears on the engine and frame. Acrid fumes from the ruptured gas tank drifted in the light evening breeze.

"Oh, that's not because of Vivian. That's because you got in my way, Goose. Well, partly because you got in my way. And partly because you're such an offensive asshole."

He sneered. "You'll be lucky to see the weekend, Clyde. You're dead meat."

I shot him in the left ankle. The blast knocked him down like it was supposed to do. It also made him noisy, which I thought was over-reacting. After all, I skipped the load off the pavement and he wore heavy motorcycle boots. He probably didn't even have any broken bones.

When Goose stopped screaming, I leaned over him and jabbed the shotgun into his crotch. "Goose, I'm ashamed of you. It's time you learned about the real world."

"You shot me, man!"

"Of course, I shot you! What did you expect me to do, fall down and whimper because you threatened me? It's very simple, Goose. Threat, click, boom. Hell, I gave you a break because I figured you were only shooting off your fat mouth. Otherwise, it would have been click, boom, dead.''

I dropped a book of matches onto his chest. "Goose," I said, "light the bike."

"Fuck you, Clyde. That's my hog! I ain't gonna burn it."

I stirred the Ithaca's muzzle around in his groin. "You really want to sing soprano at your age?"

He whined a lot, but he ignited the matchbook and threw the mini-torch at his Harley. The spilled gas caught with a fine loud *whoosh*. Goose and I stepped—well, I stepped, he sort of scuttled—away from a blazing tributary.

The burning motorcycle cast shifting smoky shadows on the surrounding buildings. A car on a cross street a block away stopped, then accelerated away.

"Okay, Goose old buddy," I said, "there's only one more chore for you. Go back to the Dew Drop and tell Fran you don't care if she talks to me. Do that tonight. Now."

He gestured at his foot. "I can't walk, you crazy bastard."

The boot did look pretty scarred up. And his foot was apparently tender. He screamed loud enough when I kicked it.

"It's not easy to get your attention, is it?" I said. "Goose, you're a DeathStar, remember? You're so tough, you can hop four blocks easily. I'll even help you up."

I thought Goose might try something when I tugged him upright, but the instant of muscle tension passed. When he was standing up, back-lit by the burning motorcycle, he seemed shorter than before. He gingerly put some weight on his left foot and swayed, breathing noisily.

"On your way, DeathStar. Tell Fran like I said. I'd give you a lift, but I don't have time. Got to find a McDonalds before they close."

When I idled past Goose sixty yards later, he was moving well enough. He was getting almost three feet to the hop, except when he overbalanced and waved his arms too much.

Eight blocks away, I passed a fire engine going toward the cul-de-sac. The men in the funny helmets looked very serious.

Personally, I thought it was funny as hell.

CHAPTER EIGHT

The next morning, at Hilda's house in Richardson, I made breakfast. Scrambled eggs with Mexican hot sauce, whole wheat toast, and coffee. I took the tray back to the bedroom, woke Hilda again, and handed her a plate. "Drop your cocks and grab your socks, we're moooving out!"

"I beg your pardon?" she said.

"That's an old military wake-up call. Barracks humor."

"It does not translate well. There is a definite problem with gender."

"True. I wonder what they say now, what with women soldiers and all?"

"I shudder to think," Hilda said, and forked up a mouthful of eggs and jalapeño peppers. She could wake up one minute and start eating the next. Without having coffee first or anything. It was awe-inspiring.

"Let me get this straight," she said. "Last night, you shot a Hell's Angel and burned his motorcycle so a stripper would tell you about the gang. Do I have that right?"

"Sort of. He wasn't a Hell's Angel; he was just a local numb-nuts. I only shot him a little bit; nothing serious. And the girl isn't a stripper; she's more like a trainee drink hustler. Basically, however, you got it right."

"Oh, well, that explains everything," Hilda said. "Wouldn't it have been simpler to talk to the woman when

48

the biker wasn't around? And where's my coffee? Oh, thanks."

"Raising hell is a basic fact-finding technique. It always helps to thrash around in the bushes, throw rocks, and holler. It makes people nervous. Now, something will happen. And, of course, I'll be able to talk to Fran without having to smell Goose in the background."

Hilda clunked her coffee cup down on the bedside table. "You don't think you've scared off the bikers, do you?"

"Jeez, I hope not. Old Goose did look a touch tight around the eyes toward the end, but I figure he'll get his nerve back, or at least his buddies will, and they'll come to me. Much easier than looking for them."

"Sir Rafferty, one of these days you're going to annoy the wrong dragon and get your butt kicked all over the castle." She said it in a joking manner, but her eyes didn't see the humor.

"I try not to think about that, love."

"Me, neither."

"I have to run, Hil," I said. "I want to be in the office when Fran calls." I kissed her good-bye, then stopped in the bedroom doorway when she slipped out of bed and padded, naked, toward the bathroom. "Hey, good-looking," I called. "If the antique business ever folds up, I know where you can get a job hustling drinks."

Hilda made a rude noise and slammed the bathroom door. I went to work.

My office was on the second floor of an old building on Jackson Street, near Harwood. A radio station had occupied the building at one time. When the media mouths moved out, the owner rented each office separately.

We were a mixed bag of lower-middle-class self-employed. There was a Greek who ramrodded a gang of door-to-door aluminum cookware salesmen, a PR man with big brass letters on his door and no clients, a two-gal secretarial service, that sort of thing. We had a bail bondsman for a while, but it was too far from the jail, so he moved.

My office had been the radio station control room, where all the red-hot sounds blasted out for Big D's rockin' robins, hey, hey, hey. The room was strangely shaped and barren, but I didn't need much. A desk, a phone, a jug of coffee, and me, so to speak.

Honeybutt was working at her desk when I sat down and put my feet up. Honeybutt was the secretary for an insurance agent next door. His office had been the radio station newsroom. There was a large plate glass window between our respective workstations, as we modern business types say. There were drapes on the insurance side of the window, but they were always open.

The floor level in my office was raised, so I looked down at Honeybutt. It was a worthwhile vantage point. In the summer, she wore short skirts. In the winter, she favored tight slacks. Her file cabinets were against the far wall and Honeybutt quite often needed things from the bottom drawers.

I never knew Honeybutt's name. We winked a lot, but we had an unspoken agreement not to talk to each other. It would have ruined the relationship.

My phone rang at 10:23. "DeathStar Stompers, Incorporated," I said. "Service with a smile guaranteed."

"Mr. Rafferty?"

"Yup. I thought about changing it to Mean Machine, but that's already been used."

"This is Fran Rosencrantz."

"Fran who?" I asked.

"Fran Rosencrantz. You gave me your card last night."

"Sure. Only, I thought your name was Zifretti."

"I don't want anything from that creep, especially his name. What happened to Goose?"

"Must have fallen off his bike. You know how dangerous those things are."

"Yeah," Fran said. She sounded tired. "So, if you want to talk, I guess it's all right."

"Good girl. Where are you?"

She gave me an address in Oak Cliff. I told her I could be there in thirty minutes. She said okay and yawned in

my ear. I didn't complain; I know show business people
are late sleepers.

The address turned out to be a white frame house in an
older, quiet neighborhood. It was a small, neat house with
a porch. The lawn was very green. Put a grinning kid
and a soppy-looking hound on the front steps and you'd
have a 1953 *Saturday Evening Post* cover.

Fran had told me her place was around the back and so
it was. She heard the car, apparently, because she came
out onto a tiny landing where a set of white wooden stairs
topped out at an apartment over the garage. She wore tan
jeans and a loose blue shirt that looked like a man's but
buttoned like a woman's. She looked different with clothes
on; crisp and housewifey.

Fran had perked up since we had talked on the telephone. She bustled me into the apartment and clattered
around the kitchen brewing coffee. She made kissy-kissy
noises while she fed a canary in a wooden cage. She served
the coffee in china cups with saucers. The cups had blue
flowers on them. She arranged a dozen Oreos on a plate
with a similar pattern. She was domestic as all get out.

We sat on a slipcovered couch in the cramped living
room. "Nice place, Fran," I said. It was true.

"Thanks. The Jamisons are sweet people. Most of the
furniture is theirs. Oh, hey, they wouldn't want to rent to
a . . . see, they think I work nights at the phone company.
I mean, I don't suppose you'll meet them, but just in case,
huh?"

"No sweat, Fran."

There was one of those supermarket decorating and rec-
ipe magazines on the coffee table. I gestured at it and
looked around the apartment. "You've done a good job.
Congratulations."

She nodded. "I'm trying. After eight years of living like
a retarded junior high schooler, it's not easy, but I'm
trying."

"I'll bet. Look, Fran, as I said last night, I don't want
to give you any trouble. I do need your help, though. What
can you tell me about the DeathStars?"

"What about them?"

"Well, anything about them. I'm just getting started. All I know about bikers is that they look bad and smell worse."

"You got that right. It's a crazy game they play. The club is everything, you see, and they have these elaborate rules about sticking together. They think it's them against the world."

"What do they have against bathing occasionally?"

"Oh, that's part of it. They call themselves outlaws. They're sure people hate them and are scared of them. Being dirty and crude and ugly makes that happen."

"You don't sound like anyone I'd expect to see on the back of a bike."

"Thank you, sir," she said, putting too much garden-party lilt in her voice.

"Big change in your life, I suppose?"

She bobbed her head earnestly. "You can't imagine. I feel like I don't even know Fran Zifretti anymore. She was somebody else. Does that make sense?"

"I think so. How did you get involved with them?"

"Long story," she said. "I got into trouble as a kid. Which wasn't surprising, now that I look back. My folks split up when I was ten and Mom worked hard at drinking herself to death. From the time I was thirteen, I did my own thing. Well, one of my own things was shoplifting. I got caught too many times, so I spent a year and a half in reform school. They called it corrective education or some such, but it was still the slammer to me. After I got out, I met Tony. By then, Mom was so far in the bottle I couldn't stand to be around her. So Tony and I got married."

She was silent for a moment. Then she shook her head.

"Wow," she said, "what a couple of dummies. We rode his bike to Bossier City, Louisiana, and found a JP. Everything was going to be terrific, we thought. Tony had a job in a gas station and—oh, I don't know, I suppose we were just playing grown-up."

"It happens fairly often. Sometimes it works."

"Yeah. Well, it didn't work for us, though it took a while to go sour. You see, when I met him, Tony hung around with a bunch of guys about his age—eighteen. Most of them had jobs, but not very good ones. Bagging groceries, pumping gas, washing cars—that sort of thing. Some of them still lived with their parents. Everybody rode bikes, though, and they started a club.''

"The DeathStars," I said.

"Oh, no, not then," she said. "It was just a bunch of kids with bikes and leather jackets, you know? Even so, it wasn't the best thing to happen early in a teenage marriage. The club took a lot of Tony's time. I was a little jealous, but it wasn't too bad. There were other girls involved. Girlfriends of the guys. We'd ride around, party, race through drive-ins. You know, kid stuff. Then Guts Holman showed up." She offered me the plate of Oreos and took one herself.

"The way you say that makes it sound like Holman suddenly dropped out of the sky," I said. "Where did he come from?"

"I don't know for sure. There was a story that Guts had been a Bandido. They're a club in Houston. Big. Bad, too. The story was that Guts had been a Bandido officer and he quit or got kicked out or got away during a bust. Or something. But I don't know about that. Guts liked to keep people guessing. He could have started that story around."

"Okay. What happened after Holman hit town?"

"Guts took over the club. Tony and the other guys thought he was a tin god, what with him being an ex-Bandido and all. Guts taught them how to organize the club and he came up with the DeathStars name."

"*Star Wars* fan, was he?"

Fran shrugged. "Maybe. Who knows? Anyway, things changed. Guts was club president, and the club got bigger because Guts brought in a whole new crowd. Older guys. Different guys."

"Like Goose."

"Exactly," she said. "Like Goose. Tony thought it was great. He wanted to be an officer, but Guts said he wasn't ready yet. Guts said Tony had to grow up, quit the kid stuff. And Guts made all the guys earn their DeathStar colors.''

I must have looked blank, because she said, "Their colors. The vests. The badges. He made them do things to earn the right to wear them."

"What do you mean? Initiations, hazing? That sounds like kid stuff to me."

"No," Fran said. "Things for the club. Sometimes they fought with other gangs. Or they robbed 7-Eleven stores. Sometimes they had to pick up packages at the air freight terminal and deliver them to a house in South Dallas. It was drugs, I'm sure. Had to be. Some of us girls didn't like that very much, but Guts turned part of the money back into the club treasury, so the guys thought it was great. Oh, and they'd boost cars, too. Never bikes—Guts wouldn't allow that—but he had contacts to get rid of cars. They hijacked a truck once, but I guess they almost got caught, because they never did that again."

"What did you think about the new club?"

"I didn't like it at all. Tony and I argued a lot, because I saw what it did to him. I mean, the club had always been important to him, but after Guts came, the club took over his life. We never did anything unless it involved that damned club."

Fran pursed her lips thoughtfully. "That was bad enough. What was strange—and scary—was how the guys changed in the way they thought about us girls."

"How was that?"

"We weren't people anymore. Just things. They had all these rules about protecting their women and not messing with each other's girls. Things like that. But the rules weren't really to protect us, the rules were there because we were . . . property, if you see what I mean."

I sipped the last of my now-cool coffee, snagged an Oreo off the plate, and wondered how feminism had missed the vast untapped market of motorcycle gangs.

"Look," Fran said, "I'll give you an example. I was always pretty flat up top, right? Tony used to tease me about it. At first, that was all right. We were newlyweds and people get goofy then. Silly private jokes and games. Tony called me 'Tiny Tits,' but I didn't mind because it was, oh, I don't know, tender. In a way." She sighed. "Then, after the club changed, it wasn't so tender anymore. And one day Tony told me they'd had a meeting and the guys had offered to let him do the next three airport pickups—and keep some of the money—so he could buy me a present. A couple of weeks later, he took me to a doctor. I came back with these." Fran waved her hands at her improbable breasts. "Charming, huh?"

"Like buying new headlights for his bike, eh?"

She finger-combed her red curls and went on. "Yeah, but I had it better than some. I think it was because Tony and I were married. And Guts liked Tony a lot. Some of the other girls—wow, they got treated like dirt."

"Worse than a mail-order chest?" I said.

"A lot worse. There was one time," she said, "when the guys came out of a club meeting and Guts went straight to Wendy Cannon. She was a young girl, kind of fat, but pretty, you know? Anyway, she was Turkey Ludder's girlfriend. And Turkey's best buddy—a greaseball named Mack—wanted to share Wendy. Turkey didn't care, apparently, so Guts okayed it. Wendy cared, though, and she said no. That was a big mistake. Guts ripped off her clothes and told Mack to jump on her bones."

Fran grimaced. "Mack did it right in front of everybody. God, it was terrible. Wendy cried and screamed and the guys cheered Mack on. After it was over, they had another meeting and voted to give Mack a special badge."

"Great friends you had, Fran."

"I know," she said, "but—hey, nothing like that ever happened to me. Honest!"

"I believe you. Next question. You seem like a decent sort. When all that mindless garbage started, why didn't you get out?"

She folded her hands in her lap and rubbed her thumbs together. She studied them intently to make sure she was doing it correctly.

"I've thought about that a lot," she said. "I left after

Guts got killed, when the club stalled for a while. I told Tony to get lost, I filed for divorce, the whole bit. I should have quit sooner, but I didn't. And the only reason I can think of . . . it was . . . I'm ashamed to admit it, but it was easier not to.''

She snuffled and turned to look at me. Her face was blubbery and soft. She looked very pretty at the time and I wondered why I had thought she was plain.

"Isn't that a helluva thing?" she said. "I let myself be like that because it was *easier*!"

CHAPTER NINE

Fran fished a tissue out of her shirt pocket. She honked and sniffed and waved her arms helplessly when I gathered up the coffee cups and carried them to the kitchen.

I poured myself another cup and sipped it while leaning against the kitchen counter. In the other room, Fran's snuffles and gulps slowly receded. Eventually, I fixed her a second cup and went back to the couch in her cramped, tidy living room.

She was ready to talk again. I asked her about the weekend when Vivian went away with the DeathStars and didn't come back.

"Look," she said, "I don't know what the deal is. She might be your girlfriend or something. Even so, you should know that nobody liked her. No offense."

"No," I said. "I met her once when she was a kid, that's all. Go ahead."

"Okay, then. Well, I don't know how she and Guts got together, but they weren't friends, either. Guts said she was studying us, and that was probably right, because that's how she acted. I don't know what she said to the guys, but she asked us girls all sorts of dumb questions. She wanted to know our roles in the . . . I think she called it the tribal society."

"Figures," I said.

"I had the feeling she thought she was in a zoo, if you can imagine that. She wanted to watch the animals and write everything down in her little notebook, so she could tell her la-de-da friends about the weird monkeys. Do you know what I mean?"

"I've met sociologists. I know."

"Okay, but what she didn't know was that she was just as weird to *us*. We laughed at her and made up crazy stories. We told her what she wanted to hear. It got to be a game."

"Margaret Mead in Samoa," I said. "It's been done before."

"What?" When I shook my head, she continued. "So, like I said, it was a game. Freak-out-the-rich-bitch. We went up to Sherman and hassled a drive-in to scare the straights and impress what's-her-name. Then we rode out to the lake. We crashed a fancy country club, but they threw us out. The manager called the sheriff and everything. So, we camped in a picnic area on the lake shore. It was pretty. That's a big lake, you know. Peaceful."

"Was that where you met the other bikers?"

"Yes," Fran said, "but that was later. After Guts got . . . uh, Vivian, high."

I sighed. "She hasn't come down yet, Fran. What happened?"

"We were loafing around the picnic area. Guts always made sure there was plenty of beer and grass, so people sat around drinking and smoking. There had been a family swimming there, but they left right away. A couple of the guys were on their bikes; doing doughnuts, practicing wheelies, that sort of thing.

"And there was an initiation. They made the new guy take off all his clothes and lie down on his back. Then the other guys stood around him and they—never mind what they did, it was pretty gross." She shook her head and grimaced. "I haven't thought about that for a long time," she said. "God, I can't believe those guys."

"Vivian," I said. "Vivian and the other bikers."

"Right. Well, some of it I saw at the time and some I

found out later, but what happened was this. Guts had a bag of pills. Uppers, downers, reds, yellow-jackets, you name it. He put a handful of them into a beer he gave to Vivian. She got pretty loopy. I remember she staggered around talking to people and writing in her notebook, only she tried to write with the wrong end of her pencil. She was really out of it.''

"Which vastly amused the assembled multitude.''

"Sure,'' she said defiantly. "And I thought it was funny, too. Not now, damn it, now I know it was dumb and cruel. But the only way I can handle this is to be straight with myself about those days. I don't fool myself anymore.

"Look, Rafferty, I'll tell you what happened, because it helps me a little to pick at that scab, but you lay off the smart-ass cracks! Or you can fuck off out of here and not come back!''

"I think you'll make it, Fran,'' I said. "I apologize. No more smart-ass cracks.''

"Hey,'' she said. "I'm sorry, too. And pardon my language. Just let me tell it, okay?''

She rubbed the back of her neck and rolled her shoulders. "The bikers who took Vivian showed up just before dark. We heard them coming. Guts hollered at everybody. We girls hid and our guys got their guns out. I thought there was going to be a fight. Then Guts recognized one of the other bikers and they started talking. Sort of strained at first. You know how dogs walk around each other when they first meet? With their bodies stiff and their hair up? It was like that. After a while, though, Guts and the outlaws were slapping each other's backs, and laughing and drinking together.''

"Did you hear any names?''

"Umm, let me think. One was called Turk, I remember that. He was the one Guts recognized. And another was named Smokey.'' She bit her lip daintily. "Smokey something; I don't know what the rest was.''

"Smokey Joe?''

"Maybe. I'm really not sure.''

"That's okay,'' I said. "What did they look like?''

"The Smokey guy was a typical biker. Fat, long hair, beard. He had a gold earring. Turk was strange; really unusual for an outlaw. He was tall, even taller than you are—which is going some—and he had big muscles like a weight-lifter."

"Most weight-lifters look fat, even if they're not."

"Well, not a weight-lifter, then. He was like the men in health studio ads on TV. Turk had muscles you could see. And he wasn't hairy. He didn't have a beard or moustache and his head was shaved. I remember it was shiny in the firelight."

"That's two." I said. "What about the others?"

Fran shrugged. "They looked like bikers. What can I say?"

"Okay. Tell me about their clothes. Were they wearing—what did you call them? Colors?"

"No. That was strange, too. They were dressed like outlaws and they rode Harleys, but they didn't wear colors."

"Does it matter what kind of bikes they rode?"

"Oh, sure," she said. "No outlaw would ride anything but a Harley."

"Goose didn't wear his colors in the Dew Drop Inn last night. He left his vest hanging on his bike outside. Could that have happened with the five bikers at Lake Texoma?"

"No, she said positively. "In the first place, the boss calls the cops if bikers wear their colors in the Dew Drop, which tells you how weak the DeathStars are right now. Secondly, that night at Lake Texoma, I saw the outlaws ride up and stop. And, anyway, they wore vests, but they didn't have any badges sewn on."

"Is there anything else about them you can remember?"

"Umm, not that I can think of." She slapped her thighs. "Hey, I'm starving. You want some lunch?"

"Okay."

"The only thing is, you caught me too early on shopping day. Would you mind going out to pick up a loaf of bread? I should be okay for everything else, if sandwiches are all right."

"Don't bother fixing anything. I'll get hamburgers. Or chicken. Or whatever."

"Oh, great," she said, hopping up. "Chicken, please. There's a Kentucky Fried about eight blocks down and two over. And I'll make a salad."

"If you'd rather, we can go out."

"No," she said. "Let's eat here." She grinned like a little girl. "I'm more comfortable in my nest. I like to play house."

The Colonel's troops loaded me up with chicken and I stopped at a liquor store for a cold six-pack. I drove back toward Fran's apartment feeling mellow and avuncular.

Hilda had often accused me of having unusual priorities. Perhaps she was right. The night before, I hadn't particularly enjoyed boozing with Fran Rosencrantz when she was near-naked in a dark bar. Now, I found myself looking forward to a scratch meal where she would be fully clothed in her homey little apartment.

Well, I was looking forward to it until I turned into the driveway and saw a big black motorcycle parked at the foot of her steps.

CHAPTER TEN

My shotgun was in the trunk. It was clean and loaded and pure hell on DeathStars. Then I thought about how it could mess up Fran's apartment.

I settled for the jack handle. And my car gun, a fine old Colt military automatic.

Moderation in all things, I always say.

My sneakers squeaked on the painted wooden steps as I climbed up to Fran's door. Sneakers, not jogging shoes. Occupational jargon.

There were four glass panes in the top half of the door. Fran and the biker stood in the kitchen. He was in his early twenties, with dark hair. He was cleaner than Goose and a lot neater. He wore new jeans and a short-sleeved white shirt. He waved his arms when he talked.

Fran's kitchen had a small Formica serving counter and she stood behind it, opposite the biker. Her face was pale and her eyes were large and round. She held a long kitchen knife in her right hand. She looked shocked, not frightened, and she didn't seem to be holding the knife defensively. And she had mentioned salad. Still . . .

The young guy jabbered away like a nervous salesman, his words muffled and indistinct through the closed door. I wondered if there was more mileage in watching or interrupting. Decisions, decisions.

Finally, he stopped pacing and waving and he started around the kitchen counter toward Fran.

That seemed a good time to interrupt.

I left the Colt tucked in the back of my belt and I walked in carrying the jack handle. "I'm home, honey," I said.

Fran eek-ed and jumped back. The knife clattered onto the counter. The kid whirled around. He looked excited, not dangerous.

Fran leaned against the sink with her right hand flat on her chest in that "you startled me" gesture only women use. "Rafferty!" she said. "Don't do that!"

The kid's eyes lit up like he had won a season ticket to the motorcycle races. "Hey, wow," he said. "You're the guy who did that to Goose? All right!"

I nodded at him and spoke to Fran. "I take it we're all friends here?"

"Of course," she said. "What's that? Did you have a flat tire?"

I laid the jack handle on the counter. "I hate to hit people with my hands," I said. "Contrary to what you see in the movies, it's awfully hard on knuckles."

The kid was pretty impressed by that. He did thirty seconds of "wows" and "all rights." Plus arm waving. Considering his dark hair and windmill imitations, his last name had to end with a vowel.

Fran frowned. "Joe told me you . . . But why . . . ? Oh, Joe's bike!" She smiled smugly. "But what if he had a gun?"

"Then," I said, "I would have played my castanets for him. Music soothes the savage beast and all that."

They both looked puzzled until I showed them the Colt and shook it. It rattled; all those mass-produced military pieces do.

I was showing off, I suppose, or maybe, as Hilda claimed, I haven't grown up in many ways. Take your pick. No fair choosing both answers.

Before Joe, the kid biker, could start up again, I sent him down to the car for the chicken and beer. He called me sir when he left. It made me feel battle-scarred. And old.

We attacked the Colonel's chicken, Fran's salad, and my beer at a matchbook-sized pine table between the kitchen and the living room. Between bites, I heard about Joe.

He was Joe Zifretti, the younger brother of Fran's ex-husband. He loved motorcycles, hated outlaw bikers, and didn't get along with his brother any better than Fran did.

"Joe heard about Goose," said Fran, "and he came to see if I was okay." She wiped her lips, smoothed her napkin into her lap, and looked at me steadily. "You didn't tell me you beat up Goose last night."

Joe Zifretti clicked his tongue and shook his head in a "wow" gesture. In a dark room, he would have been speechless.

I shrugged.

"And you burned Goose's bike," Fran said.

"*He* burned his bike," I said. "However, I did suggest to him the act might please me."

Joe's eyes clicked back and forth. Wimbledon front row. If his mouth hadn't been busy chewing, the noise would have been unbearable.

"You're not so different from Goose, then, are you?"

"Wrong," I said. "I am not fat, merely robust. I brush my teeth regularly and bathe when the need arises. I don't wear *anybody's* colors. And, cross my heart, Miss Priss, I never sold a blonde in my whole entire life. Which brings us back to the point: what happened to Vivian after Turk, Smokey Joe, and the others arrived?"

"Men!" Fran said.

"It's hell, ain't it? So tell me about it."

She helped herself to more carrot salad before she spoke. "As I said, Vivian was pretty high from the pills Guts gave her. After things calmed down—when Guts and the others were talking and drinking—Vivian stumbled over to them. I wasn't close enough to hear everything they said, but I think they were annoyed. I remember Wendy and I watched for a while, because we thought Fancy-Pants was going to get hers. But she didn't. Guts let her sit down with them.

He patted her shoulder like you would pat a dog. Friendly, but like he owned her.''

"The more I hear about this Holman scumbag," I said, "the happier I am that truck got him."

Joe mumbled around a chicken leg. It sounded like "you got it." Or something similar.

"Okay," I said. "I get the picture, Fran. What happened then?"

She shrugged. "Not much. After a while, our guys—the DeathStars—came around and told us to go to bed. Guts wanted to talk to Turk and Smokey Whatsit and the others, alone. So Tony and I went to sleep. The last I saw, Guts and the outlaws were still sitting around the fire, talking."

"Was Vivian Mollison with them?"

"Oh, yes. I think she was asleep on the ground next to Guts. At least, she looked asleep." Fran put her fork down. "That was the last time I saw her."

"When did the outlaws leave?"

"Sometime in the middle of the night. Their bikes woke me and I got up to go to the bathroom. When I went back to bed, I could still hear them a long way off."

"What happened the next morning?"

"First thing, Guts called all the guys around for a meeting. They made sure none of us girls were close enough to hear."

"Presumably, that was when Guts told them he had sold Vivian."

Fran nodded. "But, look, I can't prove that. I'm pretty sure he sold her, but I'm really only guessing from what happened after the meeting."

"Give me a fr'instance," I said.

"Well, we never saw Vivian again. That was the most obvious thing. And the guys acted funny, like little kids with a secret. They wouldn't tell, but they were ready to bust. They made jokes about the going price for college girls and whether it was better to sell one complete or a piece at a time. Dumb stuff like that."

"Any idea how much money was involved?"

Fran shook her head. "No. And Guts didn't share it with the guys, I don't think. Joe, do you know?"

Joe Zifretti choked on a bite of chicken and dropped the drumstick like it was hot. Then, with his hands empty, he could talk. "Christ, no! I only heard the story later, on the street. Somebody said five hundred dollars, but somebody else said seventy-five. And another guy said he heard a thousand."

He knocked over a salt shaker. Fran's table wasn't big enough for three people if one of them was an arm-waver. "Street talk," said Joe. "You know how it goes. You can hear anything."

"One of the things I heard indicated the outlaws who bought Vivian were from Oklahoma," I said. "What do you know about that?"

Joe twisted his lips and said, "That's nothing. Me—I heard Oklahoma, Louisiana, and Arkansas, plus San Antonio, Odessa, Lubbock, even Mineral Wells, for God's sake. I don't believe any of it. Thing is, see, outlaws don't hang around any one place unless they're in a club. Okay, they might move into somebody's territory for a while, but they won't stay too long, because the local club will run 'em off. Hell, those guys could be anywhere in the country by now."

"Maybe so," I said. "Now tell me how you fit in between sister-in-law Fran and brother Tony. You see, Joe, if you're keeping tabs on Fran for the DeathStars, I will be very angry about it."

"Hey, no way!" Palms out, fingers spread, wide eyes, and a touch of urgency in his voice. Joe Zifretti was a study of innocence. "See, that's the problem! To the average person, everyone who rides a bike is an outlaw. We all get blamed because of a few sleazy guys like Guts Holman."

"Not to mention your brother."

"Okay, okay. That's fair enough, Mr. Rafferty, but Tony and I don't get along. We never have. Fran can tell you that."

Fran continued to crunch her salad. I had long since

given up. There's a limit to how many carrots a man can eat at one sitting.

"Joe's right," Fran said. "He's been very sweet to me since I left Tony. Don't be so macho and over-protective, Rafferty."

"Congratulations, Joe," I said. "The vote is two to nothing—with one abstention—that you're a good-guy biker, not a bad-guy biker. Maybe so. Still, you showed up too soon for me. Twelve hours after I play patty-cake with Goose, you rush in here to tell Fran about it." I smiled at him. "Reassure me."

"Mr. Rafferty, everybody in town is laughing about that. After all, Goose isn't very popular. He's mean as a snake; he's stomped lots of guys. So when you took him like you did, well . . ."

Even if you gagged him, Joe would never be at a loss for words. His hands kept talking long after his mouth took a break.

"All right," I said. "I'm the new street legend. A one-man A-Team. I'll try not to let it go to my head."

"Mr. Rafferty," he said, "what did you really do to his foot?"

"Shotgun. But it was only birdshot. I made sure he didn't get one of the buckshot rounds. I don't know why everybody acts like I went after him with a goddamned flame-thrower."

Joe whistled and flipped his hand like he was shaking water off his fingertips.

Fran frowned. She asked, "Did Goose have a gun?"

"If he did, I didn't see it."

"Then, it wasn't a fair fight, was it?"

"Fair, schmair," I said. "Why this preoccupation with a fair fight? And what does 'fair' mean? Should we have been so evenly matched we killed each other simultaneously? Hell, Goose knew what was happening. He wouldn't have agreed to fight unless he thought he had an edge. For that matter, neither would I. My edge was bigger. I won. Simple."

Joe shook more imaginary water off his fingertips.

Fran said, "But—"

"But nothing," I said. "You show me a man who always fights 'fair' and I'll show you a man who loses too often. Rafferty's Rule Twenty-three."

Fran and Joe went back to eating. Fran watched her plate. Joe watched me. It was embarrassing.

I cracked another beer and lit the pipe and thought about bikers and things.

"Joe," I said after five minutes or so, "my usual snitches aren't into the motorcycle scene, but you are. How about putting out the word for me?"

If he had been a dog, he would have wagged his tail. "Sure. You bet. What?"

"Let it get around that I'm after the five outlaws Guts Holman met at Lake Texoma last year. If they're hanging around Dallas, let's smoke them out. And you can tell people I'll pay for information."

"Okay," Joe said. "And I can tell you things now. Where Goose hangs out, that sort of stuff."

"No, thanks. I already had Goose. You could probably put me onto Tony, too, but I don't want him, either. And let's keep Fran out of it. It's not her problem. Just help me find the five who bought Vivian without having to fight every biker in town, okay?"

"Oh. Yeah. Right."

I gave Joe a card. "Call me here if you get anything. How do I reach you?"

"I don't have a phone where I live. You can catch me at work, though." Joe pulled the evening shift at a twenty-four-hour convenience store near Love Field. I jotted down the address and phone number.

Fran cleared the table and started making "time to go shopping" noises, so Joe and I left. Fran followed us outside. Joe took off first, blipping his motorcycle's throttle but riding sedately enough. I put the jack handle away, shoved the Colt into the glove compartment, and started the Mustang. Then I shut it off again and got out of the car.

"Fran," I said, "this is none of my business, so tell me to butt out if you want."

She folded her arms and looked at me with a neutral expression. "Go ahead."

"Well, hell, you seem like a nice person. You've had your problems, but you're coming back. I can see that. You know it, too. So, why do you work in a scuzzy joint like the Dew Drop Inn?"

Fran smiled sardonically. "Because I like to eat. Don't forget, I have a police record. Juvenile, okay, but it's still a record. I left school in my sophomore year. I never worked anywhere before and I ran around with a motorcycle gang for eight years. I can't type or take dictation or spell properly. I don't know how to use a computer terminal. At times, I forget myself and say fuck. Now just where do you think I could find a decent job?"

"I don't know," I said. "But I'll work on it."

As I backed out of the driveway, she waved good-bye like a little girl.

CHAPTER ELEVEN

"The thing of it is," I said to Hilda, "she's trying to get back to a normal life, but she's stuck in that crummy job, hustling drinks, and shaking her ass for a bunch of rednecks who'd rather shoot pool and argue about trucks."

"No," said Hilda, "the thing of it is, you want me to find a job for one of your fallen sparrows. I don't see what that has to do with finding outlaw bikers, but that's what the thing of it is."

"Come on, honey. All you have to do is talk to your Chamber of Commerce buddies. Somebody must have a job for a nice girl who wants to get ahead."

Hilda tapped her fingernails on her desk. "You promise this Fran what's-her-name doesn't chew gum and act like a hooker?"

"Cross my heart."

"I bet she has big boobs."

"Hilda, I swear to God, she has the least sexy big boobs you ever saw."

"I don't intend to inspect them. I'll take your word for it."

"All she needs is a break, honey."

"Rafferty, you— Oh, all right. I'll ask around. But you have to promise me something."

"'Tis done, fair lady. Thy boon is granted unheard."

"Seriously," Hilda said. "Don't do anything foolish about those bikers." She shuddered. "I feel funny if I even see them on the freeway. How you expect . . . Anyway, be careful. Please?"

"Absolutely. No problem. And thanks about Fran."

"No guarantees, big guy, but I'll see what I can do."

"That's my girl."

On the way out of Hilda's store, I returned the favor. I didn't tease Purple Shirt about his spit curls.

The next day started all wrong. Marge Mollison phoned to tell me Vivian was missing.

By the time I got to Highland Park, Vivian had been gone forty-five minutes.

"We were out front," Marge said, "watering the flowers. There was a call for me and I went inside. While I was on the phone, Consuela looked out the window and saw Vivian getting into a car."

Consuela was the maid with the heartbreaker smile. She had not been fast enough to stop Vivian, but she said the car was a late-model green Pontiac. And she had memorized the last three digits of the license number. There had been one man in the car, she told us, an average-looking man. Like a salesman.

George was off somewhere at a meeting, doing whatever rich men without jobs do at such meetings.

"Okay, Marge," I said. "It's too low-key to be biker trouble. Would she get into a car with a strange man if he propositioned her?"

Marge nodded grimly. "Remember what I told you? If someone . . . Never mind, that's probably what happened."

"For now, let's assume so. I can make a pass through two or three of the closest motels. I might be lucky. That's the private way. If we go public, the cops will be slower getting started, but they'll do a more thorough job once they get rolling. Personally, I'd hedge my bet and go both ways, but it's your decision."

I didn't think many mothers could handle that sort of situation without wasting time with questions or recriminations.

Marge Mollison wasn't a typical mother. She chewed her lip for ten seconds, then said, "You start. If I don't hear from you within an hour, I'll call the police."

Consuela said the Pontiac had headed east, so I turned the Mustang that way and ambled along, trying to think like a horny salesman who had accidentally stumbled across the Linda Lovelace of his dreams. That, in itself, was a broad assumption—no pun intended—but I had to start somewhere.

Such hopeful drifting took me to a smattering of cheap motels near Central Expressway. I ignored the big Hilton on Central; it didn't seem likely my provisional salesman would pay Hilton room rates for a quickie with a casual pickup.

There were no Pontiacs at the first motel. At the next stop, there were two. One of them was green. Unfortunately, it was being loaded with suitcases by a middle-aged couple. The plate number was wrong, to boot.

Paydirt at motel number three. The Pontiac was parked in the middle of a string of concrete block rooms. The three doors closest to it were shut; the curtains were closed.

I went to the office to find the manager. If he was a reasonable, understanding fellow, I might explain my delicate mission in terms remotely resembling the truth.

He wasn't.

He was a stocky man with a baby-fat physique and an old-fashioned brush cut. He had forgotten everything he learned at his last Dale Carnegie course. He was snotty and secretive and generally uncooperative. So I dragged him up over the counter and we discussed the problem face-to-face. That cost him two shirt buttons and the key to Unit Eight.

Halfway across the parking lot, I had a sudden thought and returned to the office. Brush Cut stopped pushing buttons at his switchboard when I opened the door.

When I left again, I had the registration card for Unit

Eight and Brush Cut's solemn promise not to phone the police until he wanted his thumbs broken.

The motel registration said the Pontiac driver's name was John Brown. Sure it was.

The chain lock on Unit Eight's door was a useless after-thought. I only had to lean on the door a little bit before the screws ripped out of the timber frame.

Inside, Vivian Mollison was lying on one of the twin beds. John Brown was crawling on top of her, ten seconds from being in the saddle, on the job, in the nest, dipping his wick; pick your favorite euphemism. When the door frame splintered, he nearly broke his back straightening up.

I closed the door behind me. "John Brown's body lies a-moldering in the grave," I said. "Prophetic song, that one."

"Who are you?" he said weakly, trying to muster up a shred of dignity. It didn't work. He was a sallow, pot-bellied little guy with oily hair. I couldn't imagine him being very dignified under any circumstances.

"In one minute," I said, "this door will close behind you. In the meantime, you will hand me some identifica-tion, get dressed, apologize to the young lady and"—I stopped a feeble outburst with an upraised hand—"and you will not utter a single sentence without the word 'sir' in it. The minute starts now."

He wasted ten seconds opening and closing his mouth, then he said, "Yes, sir," and ripped the pocket of his trousers getting his wallet out. He handed me the wallet and pawed at the jumbled pile of clothing on the empty bed like a burrowing animal.

I removed his driver's license and tossed his wallet back to him. He dropped it and tried three times to pick it up. In fairness, it should be noted he was hopping around the room with his pants half on at the time.

"John L. Bartlett," I read. "Do you spend most of your spare time dragging young ladies off to motels, John?"

"No!" he said. "Uh, no, sir. I only asked for directions . . . And she said . . . I didn't force her, I swear I didn't. Sir!"

"Twenty seconds to go, John."

"Yes, sir!" He decided to do without tied shoes, his socks, and tie. "I'm ready now, sir. Please."

"Piss off, then."

He stopped in front of me, looked longingly at his driver's license, then tried to open the door.

He couldn't do it; his hand shook too much. I had to open it for him. He ran out with a jerky, lopsided gait and stumbled over the doorsill.

I closed the door behind him, leaned against it, and listened to John L. Bartlett, would-be stud, leave thirty dollars worth of rubber on the parking lot.

Vivian hadn't moved. Her legs were spread, her knees high, and her eyes empty. "He didn't apologize," she said in a bored tone.

"No, he didn't, did he? What do you say we forget it this time?"

"Sure," she said. "Who cares?"

Vivian was underweight, even for her lanky build. Her hipbones were too prominent and her ribs showed. She had an ugly bruise on her right thigh; it looked too yellow to be fresh, but I asked anyway.

"Did he hurt you?"

"No. He was okay." She giggled suddenly, stupidly.

"All right, then, let's go home, Vivian. Get up now. Get dressed."

"Don't you want to fuck me?"

"No. Thanks, anyway."

Vivian shrugged and slowly got off the bed. She rummaged through her clothes, found a pair of white panties, and stuck her feet through the leg holes. She stopped with the panties at knee level, though, and shuffled into the bathroom, bent over, clutching the waistband with both hands. Her scrawny backside stuck out awkwardly.

I remembered seeing my kid sister do the same thing when she was about three years old.

I found the room phone and dialed Marge Mollison. She answered before the second ring. "I found her," I said. "She's okay. We'll be back soon."

"Thank you," Marge said, and hung up.

Vivian came out of the bathroom and sluggishly continued dressing. She put on a pair of white shorts, then bogged
down trying to fasten her bra. I had to help her. While I
fumbled with stupid little hooks, she fidgeted and com-
plained.

"She makes me wear this thing," she said. "It's dumb.
Nobody wears stupid old *bras* these days."

In the end, Vivian didn't wear her stupid old bra either,
because I couldn't get it fastened and she refused to try
anymore.

She struggled into an "84 Olympic Gold" T-shirt,
wormed her feet into rope sandals, and we left. I stuffed
her discarded bra into my pocket.

Ah, the romance and intrigue of private investigation
work.

Back in Highland Park, Marge was dry-eyed and effi-
cient. She hustled Vivian off into the bowels of the big
house and threw me an over-the-shoulder "I'll be right
back" look. I waited.

Consuela padded into the kitchen and dribbled my heart
like a basketball. Her weepy smile had even more horse-
power than her dry dazzler. She also handed me the world's
most lovingly poured beer. I took a big chance and nodded
my thanks, even though my head was far too big to stay
on my shoulders.

Halfway through the beer, Marge returned, checkbook
in hand.

"Who was it?" she asked.

I handed her Bartlett's driver's license. "Horny aluminum siding salesman. Apparently, he stopped for directions. I don't know who came on to whom, though I
suppose it doesn't matter much."

"No. Where did you find them?"

"A no-tell motel the other side of Central. There won't
be any trouble. Nobody knows who she is and Bartlett
won't be back."

Marge waved the license. "Do you want this?"

"Nope."

She dropped it into a plastic garbage bin in the corner. The yellow lid flopped twice, then stopped. Good-bye, John L. Bartlett.

"Before you got there," Marge said, "had they . . . ?"

"No. Nick-of-time Rafferty, at your service."

She nodded. "Good. Thank you again. I don't think I could handle it if she got pregnant."

"You don't look too upset to me."

"You should see it from this side. Right!" she said crisply and started scribbling in the checkbook. "Will a thousand do? For the special service?"

"Forget it. It was only a little ten-minute job."

She looked to see if I was serious, then voided the half-written check. "I seem to keep saying thank you."

"*De nada*," I said. "Shouldn't you let George know she's back? Or did you already call him?"

"I didn't tell him she was missing."

It was none of my business. I sipped the beer and didn't say a word. She answered me anyway.

"Why call him out of his meeting? All he could do was worry and he does enough of that anyway. I decided to wait until I heard from you or had to call the police."

"Sure," I said, and drained the beer. "See you around, then. And, Marge, for God's sake, keep a better eye on her from now on."

When a thin-faced woman like Marge looked grim, she added new depth to the word. "Don't worry about that!" She fired up a Virginia Slim and huffed smoke at the ceiling. "This may sound ungrateful after what you just did, but do you have any progress to report?"

"No. I'm working on the problem. Hell, I may even be getting somewhere, but there's nothing to report yet."

"Isn't that unusual? The other firm George hired used to phone every day."

"You must have paid them by the day, then. Me, I'm on piecework, remember?"

"Very well," she said. "May I offer you anything? Another drink? Lunch?"

"No, thanks." I wanted to go home and take a shower. I felt vaguely dirty.

Halfway home, while fishing for my lighter, I found Vivian's bra in my pocket. I started to toss it on the backseat with the other junk, then changed my mind and stopped to drop it into a street corner litter bin.

An old lady walking a scruffy fox terrier gave me a helluva dirty look.

CHAPTER TWELVE

Remember the old cliché about a lull before the storm?

The next three days were like that. It was one of those periods where you drift along, going through the motions, wondering idly if you're making progress without being concerned one way or the other.

Later on, when the storm breaks, you wonder if there were signs you missed. At least, I did.

It wasn't that nothing happened during those three days; merely that nothing bad happened. Vivian Mollison didn't disappear again. The bikers didn't fire bomb my home, office, or car. My rent didn't go up. There were no unexpected bills lurking in the junk mail. It was peaceful as hell.

And it wasn't only me. Somehow the entire state of Texas scraped through without a political scandal, airliner crash, or nursing home fire. And apparently those clowns in Washington took a break, too. They managed to avoid giving themselves a pay raise or starting a war anywhere. I think they caught a politician with his hand in someone's pocket, but what else is new?

Like I said, it was a quiet time.

Still, quiet doesn't mean stopped. Rafferty's Rule Nine: Dull won't balance the checkbook. So I did my feeble best to keep the pot boiling.

So far, I had tied the bikers who bought Vivian to only two firm locations. Lake Texoma in Grayson County, where they got her from Guts Holman, and Daingerfield in Morris County, where they dumped her.

The name *Conover*—from Mollison's files—might be a person's name or it might refer to a little town in Dalton County, east of Daingerfield. That was a third, very iffy, possibility. And there was an indirect connection to Dallas, through the DeathStars. But I had that end covered, what with Goose limping and Joe Zifretti rumor-mongering.

Southwestern Bell pipped another digit or twelve into its gross sales column during that three days. I phoned in ads to the *Sherman Democrat*, the *Denison Herald*, and the *Daingerfield Bee*. As an afterthought, in case the town of Conover was involved, I also used the *Dalton County Telegraph*, the Christian voice for God-fearing, law-abiding East Texans, published weekly, and distributed throughout the best little county in all Texas, yowza, yowza.

The ads were simple. They said people who wanted to see an end to dirty, diseased, marauding motorcycle gangs should phone my Dallas number. Collect.

I had a feeling about the *Dalton County Telegraph*, so I let out all the stops in that ad. I blamed bikers for everything from AIDS to nuclear proliferation. I begged folks to help me stop those slavering, heathen animals. It was pretty strong.

After I phoned it in, I wondered if I had gone too far. Then I checked an old copy of the *Telegraph* in the big library downtown. On page three was an evangelical pitch more wild-eyed than mine. Bible Belt rural newspapers are like that, sometimes.

I didn't spend the whole three days playing Horace Greeley, though. One day I drove up to Grayson County to talk to the deputies who had shooed the DeathStars away from Tanglewood Country Club.

They tried to be helpful, but they weren't. One laconic giant in tan twill stirred parking lot gravel with his boot toe, spat, and reckoned, "You seen one of them bikers, you seen 'em all."

I nodded and stirred some gravel myself. With sneakers on, I didn't get the same effect.

The Grayson County sheriff was a guy about my age. He was sympathetic and interested. His dispatcher checked the log for the night Vivian was taken, then the two days before and after. There were no other calls involving bikers.

I didn't want a long drive to another probable deadend, so I phoned the Morris County sheriff's office. A droll middle-aged voice told me the deputy who had found Vivian was named K. B. Mackley.

"Old K. B. quit last month, but don't worry about that, Mr. Rafferty. He's around. This time of day, he'll be one of two places. Try the bowling alley first. If K. B.'s there, he'll be the tall ugly one shooting off his big mouth. If he's not there, try down the street at the cafe. He'll be eating a big chicken-fried steak. And talking." The voice paused, then added, "Course, wherever you catch K. B., he'll be talking."

K. B. Mackley answered the phone at the bowling alley. "I tell you true, Rafferty, I never seen the like of that poor little gal when I pulled up next to her. Nothing but skin and bone, she was. And smell? Oh, she was some kind of ripe. Like them hippies we used to get around here way back when. Hey, you don't see them hippies no more, do you? Where you suppose they went? Not that I miss 'em, mind you. Anyhow, you want to know about that Mollison gal. Well, sir, I had hell's own time getting her into the cruiser. Oh, she didn't fight or nothing. She just said—real meeklike—that somebody named Turk had told her to stay right there cause he'd come back for her. She believed that, Rafferty, she surely did. And, dammit, I nearly believed it, too, until I jawed with her awhile. It's hard to figure, but that poor little gal had been standing there all night and half the day! I got on the radio and the sherf said brang her in, so I done that. Later on, we found out who she was and called her people in Dallas. They come racing over here in a gy-normous Mercedes 'bout three blocks long. And that's all I know about it, but I'll tell you one thing for sure, Rafferty, one thing for sure. That little gal was messed up. Yessir, she was near-daid inside. In the head, you know, not beat up or nothing like that. I mean, she wasn't in bad shape, physical-like. Except for being god-awful skinny and stinking, you understand. Now, it ain't right that a purty little gal like that should get so messed up in the head and that's the truth of it.''

I thanked him and said, ''Tell me, K. B., why'd you quit working for the sheriff?''

''Aw, hell, Rafferty, it ain't much of a life, driving a cruiser around the county all day and night. I like to *talk* to people. Peaceful talk, not 'you drunk again, Leroy' and 'stick 'em up' and stuff like that. I just plain and simple got bored with it. Here now, I got me a bowling alley full of folks to pass the time of day with and the cutest little part-time bookkeeper you ever did see. My back don't hurt no more from those cruiser seats and—''

''Well, K. B., it's been great talking to you, but—''

''And there's one more thing, Rafferty. I don't tell most folks this, but seeing as how you're sort of in my old line of work, you might understand. I ain't had nobody puke in my car since I left the sheriff's office and that's the longest stretch I been smelling sweet air since nineteen and seventy-seven. And it's gonna get longer, too!''

''Live in hope, K. B. Live in hope.''

During the quiet three days, I also spent a lot of time with Hilda. One night we went to a new Indonesian restaurant downtown. We had *rijstaffel*, which sounded like a sneeze but turned out to be eleven courses of Indonesian cooking. Only one of them was rice. The food was good, especially a dish called *gado-gado*: vegetables and potatoes covered with peanut sauce. Between courses, Hil and I drank wine and held hands and grinned at each other like soppy kids. It was a terrific meal.

On the third day of that peaceful stretch, my ads ran in the out-of-town papers. I hung around the office all afternoon. I winked at Honeybutt and waited for the phone to ring. And I wondered if the ads were a waste of time. I finally decided, what the hell? If nothing else, they might start people talking and the word would filter back to the right place.

As the afternoon wore on, I hoped the word was filtering, because the phone didn't ring.

I left the office at six to meet Hilda at my place. When I got home, she was already there. She had a drink in one hand, my phone in the other, and an odd, still look on her face.

The caller was Lieutenant Ed Durkee, with a strong suggestion that I meet him at a certain all-night grocery store not far from Love Field. Immediately, if not sooner. And he told me why.

That was when the quiet three days ended. Or, to be more precise, they had ended fifty-one minutes earlier, when someone used a shotgun to remove Joe Zifretti's face.

CHAPTER THIRTEEN

Killing clerks at small grocery stores was an old and well-established practice in Dallas. Everyone had a role to play and everyone knew their lines.

When I arrived, Ed Durkee was already there. So were Ricco, a uniformed squad, an ambulance crew, and a mobile news unit from one of the teeny-bopper radio stations. The newsman and the ambulance crew lounged near the meat wagon, topping each other with gross-out stories. Ricco fussed with the lapels of his red-and-black plaid sports coat. The uniformed cops looked bored.

Ed Durkee had one of my business cards. He flicked it with a blunt finger and gave me his basset hound look.

"Is there a sudden cold breeze," I said, "or do I suspect this wasn't a typical stickup?"

"It was a hit," Ricco said. He smirked. "Blammo! Another biker eats gravel. Somewhere, Clint Eastwood's laughing."

"Shut up, Ricco," said Ed patiently. "Go pretend you're a cop."

Ricco pulled a face and glided away in his funny walk.

Ed flicked my card again. It looked abnormally small in his large hands. "Okay, Rafferty, why did Zifretti have this in his wallet?"

"Wow, a clue," I said. "Isn't this exciting?"

"Just wait, smart-ass. I'll give you exciting. Zifretti's inside. Most of his head is dripping off the ice cream machine. His pockets are inside out. The junk from his wallet is scattered all over the counter and this card was on top of the pile. So how's that for exciting?"

"Uh-oh."

"No shit, uh-oh! They didn't take the cash from the register or thirty bucks from Zifretti's wallet. Now, let's drop the wisecracks and talk about *this*!" He waved the card. I hadn't forgotten about it.

"I gave him that card, Ed. Three, four days ago. Look, I'll tell you about it—all of it—but first, who did it?"

Durkee shrugged. "Who knows? Some kid found the body when he went in for a loaf of bread or something. He ran home. Momma phoned it in."

"No wits, then?"

"I just got here, dammit. A squad's picking up the kid now. All I know so far is that an old lady waiting for a bus heard motorcycles in the alley at about the right time."

"Oh, shit. It's going down. Ed, two minutes! Be right back."

I ran to the phone booth at the curb and dialed my home number. It rang a long time. When Hilda answered, I breathed again.

"Hil, honey, listen carefully. Go home. Right now."

"I started supper. I—"

"Drop everything and get out of there, Hil. Now."

"Rafferty, what's wrong?"

"Nothing, I hope. Babe, this is important. I'll explain when you call me from your place. Please go home right now."

"This isn't a joke." Statement, not a question.

"No, Hil. No joke. I'm sorry." I gave her the phone booth number and told her to call as soon as she got home.

"Okay," Hilda said flatly. She hung up.

I hung up, too, and turned around to face the radio newsman. He was clean-shaven and blow-dried and blue-eyed and handsome as hell. He should have been on television.

He probably thought that, too.

"Uh, excuse me," he said. "I need to use the phone."

"It's not working."

"Come on, you were just talking on it! Don't you know who I am? I'm—"

"I'm the tooth fairy," I said. "Get lost."

"Now, look," he said. His voice dropped four tones. Typical radio announcer. "That is a public phone and—"

"It's private for the next half an hour, Jack. Go away."

We stared at each other for a while, then he nodded to himself and walked away. Maybe he wasn't used to an audience that looked back.

It was after seven o'clock by then. The sun was low and orangy-red on the horizon. I held the phone booth door open with one hand and leaned on the sharp aluminum frame. I tried to picture Hilda picking up her purse, leaving the house, closing the front door, walking to her car, getting in, getting away.

A squad car pulled into the lot. A fat black kid and a woman in a print housedress got out. Ed Durkee talked to the kid. The mother held her son's hand and looked wary.

Cars passing on West Mockingbird slowed down to gawk at the lights on the squad cars and ambulance, then squirted past. High tech buzzards.

Six minutes. Hilda should have been well away from the house by then.

It had become a little dimmer. It was still warm, but the heat came from the pavement and the buildings, not the sky. Gnats fluttered around the light in the phone booth ceiling. I swatted a mosquito on my left arm. It smeared.

Eight minutes.

The radio news voice sidled over to where Ed Durkee talked to the black boy. Ricco shooed the newsman away. He stalked to his gaudy station wagon and drove off. As he did, he made certain the tires squawled. He sure showed Ricco.

A uniformed cop shot him the finger. The medium is truly the message.

Eleven minutes. Hilda should have been almost home. If she had caught the lights right. Maybe she hadn't.

A new gray Oldsmobile pulled in and jerked to a halt. The tires yelped. The driver left the car door open when he got out. His face was as gray as his car. He talked to a patrolman, who talked to Ed, then took the man inside the store.

Fourteen minutes. The phone rang.

"I'm home now, big guy. What in the world is going on?"

"Remember the Zifretti kid I told you about? Somebody wasted him out here by Love Field. It may have been bikers."

"Oh, boy," she said in a small voice. "Why?"

"Don't know. Maybe because he talked about me. Or Vivian. Whatever. The point is, they must know I'm looking for them."

"Rafferty," Hilda said, "why does this affect me? No, wait, that sounds terrible. I mean, I'm sorry the boy is—"

"It's okay, babe. I know what you mean. I want you out of my place because I don't know what they'll do next. Hell, they might not even think of looking up my address. And I read or heard somewhere that bikers have rules about keeping womenfolk away from the action. Though I don't know if that applies to their opposition. I had to be sure, honey. I don't want you mixed up in this."

"There's a sweet thought in there somewhere," she said. "Scary, but sweet."

"Love you, babe. See you when I can."

"Love you, Ugly. Though I wonder why at times."

"I think it's my rugged good looks. The right profile gets you broads every time."

"Be careful. Promise?"

"Guaranteed. Bye."

I hung up and wandered off to tell all.

All the usual cop things happened. They interviewed everyone in sight, drew diagrams, took pictures; all that studious, detailed Sherlock Holmes stuff. A little after nine, they let the ambulance men put Joe Zifretti into a body bag, along with a few hundred flies.

Then we tried to put it all together.

"Okay," said Ed, "we got an armed robbery. Maybe. And maybe not, because they left the cash. We know the shooter stood there. We know they searched the body afterward, so they wanted something and they didn't panic. We think they were bikers. We think there was more than one. And we think they went out the back door." Ed sighed. "Closest thing we got to an eyewitness is the kid. He says it was about 5:45 when he got here. And supposedly Zifretti was still twitching, which is why the kid puked all over the floor there."

Ricco helped himself to a bag of Fritos from a shelf. He crunched a mouthful and said around the crumbs, "On the other hand, Zifretti wasn't twitching when the owner got here, and *he* puked over *there.*"

"So what?" said Ed. "For Christ's sake, Ricco, close your mouth when you eat. Do you know how disgusting that looks?"

"This woman who heard a bike," I said. "Could that have been Zifretti coming to work?"

"Naw," said Ricco. "Zifretti's shift started at four. Besides, the old broad is pretty certain she heard more than one bike. Could have been somebody taking a short cut, though."

"Yeah," I said. "Or maybe it was Evel Knievel practicing wheelies. Or Steve McQueen risen from the grave. Come on!"

Ed scratched a rubbery jowl. "Knock it off, you two. Unless we turn anything new, we'll figure whoever did it rode motorcycles."

"Damn right," I said. "But why? Because Joe was talking up the Mollison snatch for me? Or just pure meanness? I understand Joe didn't get along with the hard guys very well."

"Bad-mouthing the animals wouldn't buy him a face full of buckshot," Durkee said. "And besides, if his brother is into this motorcycle gang bullshit, that should have bought the kid a little protection. Most of the gangs go for that brotherhood macho crap.''

"Bear with me, Ed, I'm in devil's advocate mode,'' I said. "Maybe we're reading too much into this thing. I didn't know Zifretti very well. He might have been screwing somebody's wife or girlfriend. Or dealing coke. Or Christ knows what.''

"We'll find out about the woman angle,'' said Ed.

Ricco sneered. "Forget about the coke wet dreams, or anything else involving money. The last coke dealer I knew who moonlighted as a grocery store clerk was never.''

"I feel bad about this,'' I said. "I wouldn't have asked him to tease the animals if I'd thought they'd play Shoot the Messenger.''

"Naw,'' Ricco said around a Frito. "That ain't it. They wouldn't blast him for that. Makes more sense they smoked him cause of something he was gonna tell you.''

That was Ricco all over. He looked like a part-time pimp, but he had good instincts.

"Now, *that* I like,'' Ed said. "Rafferty?''

"Possible. Likely, even. Always assuming we're not making too much out of a holdup by a freaked-out junkie.''

Durkee arranged the wrinkles in his suit with a shrug. "If so, there'll be another one. Or the scumbag will cop to this one when we bust him next year for spitting on the sidewalk or something.''

"Or, we don't fit anybody for it ever,'' Ricco said, "for which I will give you good odds.''

"Shut up, Ricco,'' groaned Ed. "You depress me.''

"Well, you two can play it however you want,'' I said. "Me, I'm betting it was the same bikers who snatched Vivian Mollison. That's my only option. If I think anything else, it leaves too many back doors open. Which means, I have work to do. Are we finished here?''

"People of no official standing are finished here,'' said Durkee. "That means you, Rafferty. And people of high rank and experience are also finished for the time being. That's me. Sergeant Ricco, however, has paperwork to do. Right, Ricco?''

The corners of Ed's mouth came up to level. For him, that was uncontrollable mirth.

Ricco looked like someone had spit on his pretty jacket.

I wanted to go straight to Hilda's. I wanted to spend the rest of the evening holding her hand, to comfort her, and be there if she needed me. That's what I wanted to do.

But I couldn't do that. I was too worried about someone else who knew about—and hated—the big bad bikers.

I let Fran Rosencrantz's phone ring twenty times before I hung up.

When I tried the Dew Drop Inn, a nasal voice answered. The voice admitted Fran was working, but refused to let me talk to her.

"Who'd ya say this is?" Nasal Voice whined.

"Harry," I said. "I bought her a drink the other night. I think she likes me."

"Oh, yeah, sure. Well, Harry, tell you what, old buddy. She's here. She looks lonely, Harry. Whyn't ya come on over? Buy her a drink or two, she might go home with ya. After closing time, a course. How 'bout it, pal? Whadda ya got to lose?"

I wondered about that, too.

I went to the Dew Drop Inn anyway.

CHAPTER FOURTEEN

"Oh, my God," Fran said. The lighting inside the Dew Drop Inn was lousy, but it was good enough to see her face sag. "Poor Joe."

"Yeah, helluva shame," I said. "Now let's worry bout poor Fran."

"When did it happen?"

"Five, six hours ago. I got tied up with the cops for a while, and then I had arrangements to make, or I'd have been here sooner."

Chuck the bartender greased and slimed his way to our booth. He thought Fran looked thirsty again. I gave him a twenty and told him to stay away for half an hour. It was quicker than arguing.

"Well," Fran said, "I feel sick about Joe, but you're going off the deep end. Why should I run away? Besides, if I left now, I'd get fired. What would I do for a job then?"

She wore—or didn't wear, depending on how you looked at it—her working clothes. She crossed her arms over her bare plastic breasts and hugged herself. "I'm cold," she said.

It wasn't cold. I had my nylon windbreaker on, but not because of the temperature.

"You're not cold, you're scared," I said. "And you

should be. Take a look out front. Don't go outside, for God's sake, just look.''

Fran started to argue, then she went toward the front door. She wore higher heels than the first time I had seen her. The exaggerated heels made her legs look longer, and they gave her a ludicrous walk, like a parody of a street-corner hooker.

She opened the door a foot or so and poked her head out. After thirty seconds, she carefully closed the door and came back. Her face was pale.

"Oh, shit," she said. "We're fucked."

"No, we're okay. Tell me what you saw."

"They're across the street. Three of them."

"What are they doing now?"

"Standing by their bikes," she said. She gulped. "One of them waved at me." She closed her eyes and pushed her hands into her lap. Her arms were rigid. "I don't think I can take this."

"Sure you can. You have to. In a few minutes, we'll walk out of here. It'll be all right if you do what I tell you."

"That's what you say. Why don't we call the cops?" She laughed bitterly. "I never thought I'd say that, but I sure like the idea now. Let's call the cops."

"What could they do?"

"Let me get the fuck out of here alive, that's what they could do!"

"True," I said. "But they can't arrest those goons across the street, because they haven't done anything. Yet. So, afterward, after the cops leave, what will you do, Fran? Go home? Pull the covers over your head and pretend you don't hear the motorcycles coming up the driveway?"

After a long moment, she said, "You're right. What do you want me to do?" She said it dully, as if escape was so improbable a struggle didn't matter.

"When you looked outside, did you see a blue Chevy pickup parked on the right side of the lot? With a man in it?"

"Yesss," she said hesitantly. "He's thin and wearing western clothes. And a big hat. The door is open and he's sitting sideways behind the wheel, with his feet out the door. Drinking a beer." Reciting the details seemed to comfort her.

"He's a friend, Fran. You're not alone. In fact, when we go out there, everyone except the bikers will be either neutral or a friend. Remember that."

She nodded. "If you say so."

"I say so. Go get dressed now. We'll leave when you get back."

She sat for a long time without moving. I thought she was going to refuse. Then, finally, she sighed and stood and walked toward the back of the big room. After three steps, she stopped and took off her hooker shoes. She carried them while she padded down the corridor and bumped a door open with her shoulder.

She was back in six minutes, dressed in jeans and a thin, long-sleeved pink cotton pullover with a scoop neck. She wore leather sandals, the kind with a loop over the big toe, and she carried an outsized straw purse. She sat down.

"Leave the sandals here," I said. " We might have to run."

She took them off and dropped them into the straw bag. "I was thinking," she said. "You don't have to do this, do you?"

"No, I suppose not."

"I mean, those guys murdered Joe tonight."

"Well, let's be fair, Fran. We don't know for certain they did it."

"You think they did, though, don't you?"

"Oh, sure."

"So," she said, "you came to get me out of here and it's not even your fight."

"It's my fight. I want them, don't forget."

"You say that like it's a . . . a regular *job*!"

"It is. This sort of thing is part of what I do."

She shook her head. "Wow, I am really fucked up. Here

I am, arguing with you, instead of being grateful. The truth is, Rafferty, I am scared to death. Really."

"It's okay," I said. "I'm scared, too. You'll forget about it when—and if—things start to happen."

"Do you like it? Being scared and knowing there are people out there who might kill you and then going out there anyway? I read something about people like that. People who like it."

"Yeah," I said. "Yeah, I guess I do."

"Wow," she said again. "You're more fucked up than I am."

"We'll go now, Fran. Walk on my left. One step behind. That's important. No matter what I do, stay to my left and a little behind. And don't touch me or grab me. Okay?"

She nodded shortly. "Okay. Hoo-boy," she said, blowing it out in a long loud breath. "Okay."

After that, there was nothing more to talk about, so we went out.

I held the .45 behind my right thigh. When we cleared the door, I felt Fran move into position where I had told her.

Off to our right, Cowboy drained his beer and tossed the bottle into the bed of the pickup. He stretched slowly, sleepily, then turned to face the wheel. He started the pickup. He didn't close the door or switch on the lights.

The three bikers spotted Fran. They swaggered across the street toward us. Fran's description had been accurate and I recognized Turk as the one in the middle.

Turk was a big son-of-a-bitch, six-four, at least. He wore a sleeveless denim vest and his arms were corded with long ropy muscles. He looked fit and dangerous. His bare scalp gleamed in the street light. He was clean, for a biker, and he stood out in his small crowd. The other two were overweight and dirty.

The biker on Turk's left nudged him and guffawed. Turk smiled. It wasn't what you'd call a friendly smile.

When they stepped up onto the curb on our side of the

street, I started forward. Fran came along, a half beat late. She whispered softly. Over and over, she said, "Oh, shit."

The bikers were twenty yards away when Cowboy made his move.

He popped the pickup into gear and slewed it across the parking lot in front of the bikers. The Chevy squawked to a stop. The open driver's door creaked forward on its hinges. Cowboy slid across the seat and shoved a handgun with an absurdly long barrel out the passenger window. He pointed it at Turk and his playmates.

Out on the street, another pickup truck—a maroon F100—burned rubber and crashed into the three parked motorcycles. The bikes toppled like dominos, and the pickup, now in a stump-jumping low gear, roared and waddled up onto the pile.

Mimi jumped out of the truck. She had her Browning 12-gauge pump and she held it on the bikers as she ran to our left. Her boot heels clunked rhythmically on the pavement. She carefully avoided Cowboy's killing zone.

I pulled Fran forward, down and across, under my gun arm, and shoved her toward Cowboy's pickup. "Get in," I said.

It was going down according to plan; everything clicking into place, neat and orderly with the lubricant of organization and the hot sweet rush of adrenaline. What could be strange about enjoying anything like that?

It all went to hell when the other two bikers came out, one from each side of the Dew Drop Inn.

They were afoot, running, converging on the pickup. Then the one with the machete swerved and ran toward Mimi.

"On the right, Mimi. He's yours," I yelled.

I turned and shot the other biker, the one with the shotgun, high in the chest. As he went down, his weapon fired. After the echoing bark of the .45, his shotgun sounded vague, like thunder in distant hills. A two-foot wide section of the Dew Drop Inn sign disappeared. White plastic fragments drifted down onto the parking lot.

I turned again, with a vulnerable itchy feeling in the small of my back.

I needn't have worried. Mimi had the machete-waver faced down.

Cowboy hadn't moved. The barrel of his hand-cannon pointed at Turk and company like the finger of an avenging angel. They didn't move either.

I butt-bumped Fran into the center of the Chevy's bench seat and eased the pickup forward toward Mimi. The biker with the machete stood twenty feet away with his hands at his sides. He stared at Mimi and swore mechanically. "Fucking midget cunt," he said.

That was a cheap shot; Mimi wasn't *that* short.

I covered Mimi while she scrambled into the back of the truck.

The biker ignored my .45. He glared at me. "You wasted Frog," he said. "You're next." He turned and slowly walked away.

"Kill him," Cowboy said, without turning his head. The biker kept walking.

"No," I said, "we got the girl out. Let's go. Ready?"

"Making a mistake," said Cowboy. "Ready."

"Go," Mimi called from the back.

I put the Chevy in gear and we left.

Three blocks away, Fran began to cry. I patted her leg and made "there, there" noises.

Cowboy sniffed. "Pretty dull. You and Mimi had all the fun."

"Hell, you made five hundred bucks. That's not bad for thirty minutes' work."

"True," he said. "Lot of travel time, though. Especially for something this boring."

Mimi banged on the roof of the cab and shouted. I slowed down to hear her. "Biker coming up," she said.

It was Machete again, on a cut-down Harley. He pulled

alongside and took a swipe at Mimi. The long blade screeched like fingernails on a blackboard as it scraped on the edge of the pickup bed. Then it clanged against the side of the cab.

"You stupid man," Mimi said two feet behind my head. Her Browning boomed. Machete and the bike went down in a low slow slide into a light pole.

I got the pickup stopped halfway down the block and backed up. We all got out and stood under the street light around the wounded biker.

Machete was draped face down over his Harley. It looked like someone had smeared red paint over a slimy gray hose, dropped the mess on the bike, then put him on top of it all.

"Gut-shot," Cowboy said. "Mimi shoots a little low sometimes."

"Sorry," said Mimi contritely.

Machete moaned and gargled and tried to move when I searched him. I found a greasy wallet in his hip pocket.

Machete was William B. Becker. "Hey, Bad Bill," I said, "you feeling baaad tonight?"

"Goddam midget cunt shot me." He coughed wetly. He twisted his head and looked up at me. His beard was shiny where blood flowed from the corner of his mouth. "You," he croaked. "You offed Frog. Said I'd get you."

"Told you to kill him back there," Cowboy said. "Some people never listen to the hired help."

"Shut up," I said. "Bad Bill, tell me about your buddy Frog. He the same Frog from when you had the blonde college girl?"

Becker coughed blood onto his bike. "Man, Frog sure did like to jump that mama," he said dreamily. "Prime pussy, fer sure."

"You've been shot in the stomach with a twelve-gauge, Bill. You're going to die. You know that, don't you?"

Becker gargled something that sounded like yes.

"Does it hurt?" I said.

"Yeah," he gasped. "It's bad, man. Real bad."

"Well," I said, "I sure as hell am happy about that."

CHAPTER FIFTEEN

I drove the pickup to the shopping center where I had left the Mustang. Fran and I got out. She stood silently while I unlocked the car. She let me hand her into the passenger seat, tucked her straw bag beside her feet, and stared straight ahead at the dark storefronts. I closed the door. Fran locked it.

Mimi swaggered over and slapped me on the butt. "Good to see you, Rafferty," she said. "Been too long. I almost forgot how big you are, you old poop." She held her cheek up to be kissed. She stood on her tiptoes, so I didn't have to bend over any farther than at the average drinking fountain.

"Come on, Mimi. We got to go," Cowboy called from behind the wheel of the pickup. "So long, Rafferty. Let us know, you need any more help." He pronounced it *hep*.

"Midnight Lady's about to foal," said Mimi in a low voice. "You know how he is about the horses. Bye now." She climbed into the pickup cab and waved as they pulled away.

I lit my pipe while the Mustang wheezed and rattled and decided to keep running. Fran sat quietly. I tucked the .45 between my seat and the console. That seemed too melodramatic, so I put it in the glove compartment.

Fran moved her knees out of the way and turned her head to face the window on her side.

Ten blocks later, she was still studiously examining the blurred curb.

"Why, hell, lady, it wasn't anything at all," I said. "There's no need for you to thank me and carry on like that."

"I've been thinking," she said. "Before you came along, I had a job. It wasn't much, but I had a job. And a nice apartment. And people weren't trying to kill me."

"When you live in a sewer, Fran, sooner or later you get shit on your shoes. Maybe not at first, but eventually."

"Oh, great! Now it's all my fault, eh?"

"No. Not entirely," I said. "But don't forget, I didn't cause this mess. I'm only the guy trying to clean it up. Or should we let Turk and his pals find themselves another blonde?"

"No. I didn't mean it that way."

"Yeah, we could do that," I said. "Maybe next time, they'll buy a nun or a kindergarten teacher. You know, somebody who really deserves it."

"Stop it! You're twisting things."

"The hell I am. You better face up to it, kid. It's time to pay your dues. If you had started earlier, you might be finished by now. You didn't. Okay. You're working on it, though, and that's good. And you're lucky. You have me on your side and I think you're going to make it."

"If I stay alive long enough."

"Trust me."

"What's with you?" she said. "I mean, Christ, I thought bikers were mean, but . . . Except you don't come on mean."

"Just a country boy trying to get along."

She sighed. "You're not a country boy."

"True. But they say that out in the boonies and I kinda like the sound of it."

"Those people were country, weren't they?"

"Cowboy and Mimi? Yeah, they're country. Nice couple," I said.

"He reminds me of somebody," Fran said. "From an old cowboy movie, I think."

"James Coburn," I said. "*The Magnificent Seven*. Coburn said about twenty words in the whole movie."

"Are they brother and sister or what?"

"Married. She's a lot younger, though."

She recognized something a few blocks from her apartment and realized where we were. "Hey, I thought you said—"

"Take it easy. I wouldn't leave you here. Pack some clothes. Enough for three or four days."

I waited outside, sitting on the steps with the Colt in my hand. The gun smelled from when I had killed Frog. I wondered whether I really needed it, but I wasn't brave enough to leave it in the car.

John Wayne would have thrown the .45 away and taken on the bad guys with his bare fists. Take that, pilgrim. And where's the horse I'm supposed to kiss?

Such day-dreaming was pure hoke. Turk and his pals weren't likely to get organized so quickly.

Still, no one ever got hurt by being prepared for the worst. So, I sat on the hard steps and cradled the gun in my hands and looked at the stars.

Fran was fast. Inside ten minutes, she dropped a cardboard box of clothes on the landing, went back in and returned with a shopping bag and a worn canvas hold-all. "Sorry," she said. "I don't have a suitcase." She left her canary on Jamisons' porch.

We loaded her gear into the Mustang and left. She sat sideways on the seat and watched me drive. I took the Jefferson Boulevard Viaduct to Market, then turned right on Commerce. It was dark and quiet at the bottom of the concrete canyons. Peaceful.

"Where are we going?" she asked eventually.

"You'll see."

Her voice tightened. "I get it. The big man wants his reward. I get dragged back to your cave and you jump on my bones for a day or two, right?"

"No," I said. "Your relatives might hire some bad-ass to hunt me down later. Who knows where it could end?"

Hilda smiled sweetly at Fran. "Would you excuse us a moment? Rafferty, may I speak with you in the kitchen?"

Hilda crashed around, filling the pot, throwing coffee into the basket. She plugged it in and leaned against the counter with her arms folded. "Now! What's the idea dragging *her* in here in the middle of the night?"

"Hil, babe, a lot has happened you don't know about. I couldn't dump her anywhere at this hour. And I feel like a bum because I couldn't get here any sooner. Now will you please come out into the living room and let me tell you about it? After that, if you insist, we'll toss her out on her ear. Promise."

"Rafferty . . . You don't understand. I was feeling sexy and tender, waiting for you. I fell asleep thinking you'd wake me up and . . . And look at the place! It's a mess. You shouldn't have brought a woman around now."

"I've got an idea about that, too. Come on. Please?"

Over coffee, I brought Hilda up-to-date. Fran, too, though she already knew most of it. It was almost three when I finished.

"So," I said, "I think Fran should stay here for a while. Then I can keep an eye on both of you. Not that I expect any trouble. They're not likely to get any farther than Fran's place. And maybe my house."

"Rafferty," Hilda said, "what if I'm not ready for a roommate?"

"Well, I can't take her home with me. That's back into

the combat zone. So, if you absolutely refuse, Fran goes. Right now. She'll have to take her chances on the street. I suppose she could throw a brick through a jewelry store window and hope to end up in the slammer."

Fran bit her lip. "I don't like the sound of that."

"Hilda hasn't said no yet."

"No," Hilda said, "I haven't said no yet. I just hadn't realized Rafferty had settled on celibacy as a life-style."

"Ouch. Okay, listen. It's only for a few days, maybe a week. By then, it should all be over. We'll find Fran a new job, she can move back into her apartment, we're all home free."

"Suppose Hilda lets me stay here," Fran said. "What am I supposed to do for money? Though I won't need much if all I can do is lie around all day."

"No lying around for you, cookie," I said. "You want a fresh start, now's your chance. You can clean up here while Hilda's at work. Fix the meals. Things like that."

"A cleaning lady?" Fran said. "You want me to scrub toilets?"

"Whatever's needed. It pays thirty a day, plus room and board."

"Rafferty . . ." Hilda said.

"No, it makes sense," I said. "Scrubbing toilets is a step up from where she was headed at the Dew Drop Inn. And why would you turn down free maid service? I'll spring for her pay." I spread my hands like the pope at Easter. "What more could you ask?"

Fran looked at Hilda warily. "Is he like this often?"

"Yes," Hilda said. "Too goddamned often, if you ask me." She shrugged. "If we do this, you should know I don't like living with other women. So we would need ground rules. The master bathroom is mine. I have no interest whatsoever in your family photos or sex life or star sign. And if you touch my clothes or listen to rock music, it's good-bye, roomy.''

   ''Okay,'' Fran said. ''I can deal with that.''

   ''Good girls,'' I said. ''Make nice.''

CHAPTER SIXTEEN

"You let them *get away*?" Marge Mollison stubbed out her cigarette and gave me a sour you-can't-get-good-help-anymore look.

We were outside again, around the table on the Mollison patio, eating lunch al fresco like The Beautiful People. The cold ham was wonderful. The potato salad had too much dry mustard.

"They didn't get away, exactly. They're still in town, probably. Shouldn't take too long now." I tried the potato salad again. The second bite was better.

George ignored his food and toyed with a wine glass. He stared at the white metal tabletop, where Becker's wallet lay like an ugly black toad on a lace lily pad.

I nudged the wallet with my finger. "Two of them are out of the way. Becker and the one they called Frog. They're dead. Too bad you missed it, Marge."

George winced.

"You're sure this Frog person was involved?" Marge asked. She reached for another cigarette, found the pack empty, and shook a small brass bell near her place setting.

"Oh, yeah," I said. "The reports you gave me mentioned a man named Frog. And before Becker died, he said Frog had . . . um, known Vivian. That might not stand up in court, but it's close enough for me. I'm going to charge you for him.''

Marge nodded, then smiled brief thanks when Consuela put a fresh pack of Virginia Slims beside her plate. Marge opened it with taut, precise movements, used a blood-red fingernail to pry out the first cigarette, lit it, and dragged a half inch of incinerated tobacco into her lungs. "Very well," she said, "we owe you ten thousand dollars. When will you get the other three?"

"You owe me six thousand. I killed Frog because he had a loaded shotgun and the situation had turned to worms around me. I didn't have time to handle him any other way. On the other hand, Becker was just plain stupid. He forgot it's the size of the gun that counts, not the size of the person holding it."

Marge shook her head. "How and why doesn't matter. They're dead. That's what counts."

"Point is," I said, "I didn't go out to waste them because you offered a premium for scalps. They chose the way to go. You didn't, I didn't. Stop trying to buy what isn't for sale. Pass the ham, please."

George eased another slice of meat onto my plate. The serving fork clattered when he put it down.

"Rafferty," he said, "I think you know I don't care about, ah, revenge." Marge frowned at him. He went on. "Marge may feel it's . . . but I . . . I wish you could cooperate with the police on this."

He leaned forward on his elbows and I noticed again how much he looked like John Glenn. But older, even though he wasn't.

"And what bothers me," George said, "is that you probably can't do anything *except* kill them. The police aren't interested. They made that quite clear." He sounded wistful.

I nodded and swallowed. "Don't be too hard on the cops, George. They have problems, too."

Marge sniffed. Who started that old cliché about the weaker sex?

"The cops will move if we come up with evidence," I

said. "I'm working on that. I have an eyewitness who can place Turk at Lake Texoma, talking to Holman the night before Vivian disappeared. It's not airtight, but it's pretty good circumstantial evidence. Probably good enough to convict, given the lousy press the bikers get. Especially since this Turk character is bald, big, clean-shaven. He stands out. A jury would believe that sort of eyewitness testimony. The rest of it isn't so good. My witness can testify another biker was named Smokey-something, but I doubt that part will hold up. Nicknames aren't usually solid enough. And the third one—this Stomper character—well, we've got nothing solid on him."

"They run in a pack," Marge said. "Doesn't that help?"

"Some. The trouble is, the guy we can lock in—Turk— is the least likely to come in alive."

"Why do you say that?" asked George.

I finished my ham and pushed the plate away. "Nice meal. Thank you," I said. "Last night, Turk and the two who must be Stomper and Smokey Joe stared down the barrel of a Ruger Blackhawk. A friend of mine would have killed them if they'd sneezed. They knew that. It didn't bother Turk." I shrugged. "It's hard to explain if you haven't seen it. It's the way a man stands, how he holds his head, how he looks at the gun."

George moved his wine glass in small circles on a drink coaster. "You can tell that about a man by watching him?"

"Yeah," I said. "You can tell."

"What about the others?" Marge asked.

"Smokey Joe and Stomper? Typical bikers. Fat, ugly, beards. Dirty. They're tough, I think, but not as tough as Turk. Or me."

Marge kept it barely below a taunt. "Is Turk tougher than you?"

"Maybe. We'll find out."

She took another drag on her smoke without breaking eye contact. "And if you have to kill him?"

"Then I will," I said. "Nobody's tougher than a bullet."

Consuela cleared the plates and silverware away, poured

coffee all around, and replaced Marge's small ashtray with the big stone one. She also smiled at me. I winked and she dropped her eyes.

"When you're quite finished flirting with the servants," Marge said, "perhaps you'll answer George's question about getting the police involved."

I lit my pipe and let them wait. When it was burning nicely, after it was tamped and tapped, after I had done all that fiddling we pipe smokers are prone to do, I said, "Like I say, the problem is evidence. It would help a lot if Vivian could identify the bikers."

George shook his head slowly. Marge finished a sip of coffee, carefully put her cup down, and said, "Out of the question."

"You're not making it easy."

"Easy?" Marge snapped. "How easy do you think it would be for Vivian to testify? You've seen her. Can you imagine how some slimy defense lawyer would treat her?" She held her head a little sideways and pantomimed amazement. "And you didn't try to escape, Miss Mollison? Not even once in ten months? Why not? Tell the jury about your sexual experience before you seduced these men, Miss Mollison. How many lovers have you had in the past month?"

Marge dropped the act and spoke harshly. "When I was fifteen, my older sister was raped, Rafferty. She made a mistake. She reported it to the police. I still remember the trial and how they distorted things. How they called her a whore. And I remember lying awake at night, listening to Barb cry. I wanted to comfort her and I couldn't, because Barb couldn't bear to have anyone touch her. Not even me, her sister." She slapped her hand flat on the table. Coffee slopped out of the cups. "I will not put Vivian through that, Rafferty. Never!"

No one spoke for several moments. There wasn't much to say.

Consuela mopped up coffee and brought clean cups and saucers. As she poured a fresh round, a bell bonged softly inside the house.

"I'll get it," George said. "Go ahead here, Consuela."

George came back with Ed Durkee and Ricco. "These gentlemen are from the police, dear," he said to Marge.

"Well, I'll be—" Ricco said. "Look who's here." He wore a blue leisure suit with white stitching that highlighted the lapels and pockets, a pale pink shirt and white shoes.

Ed Durkee wore a brown suit. What else?

Marge, with genteel hostess noises, got Ed and Ricco seated, coffee-ed and offered them lunch, which they refused. During the to-ing and fro-ing, I slipped Becker's wallet into my hip pocket.

"Now then, Lieutenant, what can we do for you?" Marge said brightly.

"Mrs. Mollison," Ed rumbled. "Mr. Mollison. There were two shooting incidents last night that may be related to your daughter's disappearance last year."

"Oh, my," Marge said. "George, did you hear that? What happened?" Her act was as transparent as a wet T-shirt, but Ed didn't react. There's nothing like sitting across from five million dollars to curb a cop's tongue.

Ed went through the Joe Zifretti story step-by-step. Marge did a body-language number on him, with wide-eyed looks and open palms and leaning forward. George stared at the table legs. Ricco studied the house and grounds slyly, like he wondered if they would take a thousand down and three hundred a month on a conditional sales contract.

Ed said, "Your friend Rafferty here tells us he's looking for the men who took your daughter. This Zifretti was indirectly involved." He told the Mollisons about Joe and Tony Zifretti, rolled his eyes a little at Marge's overacting, and went on to Fran.

"You'll be interested in this, Rafferty," he said. "Fran Rosencrantz—the one Ricco told you about in my office—walked off from her job last night. The bartender and two of the other girls say she left with a man. Male Cauc. Six-two, two-twenty, curly brown hair. Sound like anyone you know?"

"Why, Ed, that was me! After the Zifretti hit, I was

afraid Fran might be next, so I told her about it and we got the hell out of there. Can't be too careful, you know.''

"How thoughtful of you," Marge murmured in a bitchy tone.

"Yeah, well," Ricco piped up, "about the time you left, all hell busted loose in the parking lot. This morning, we got two bikers in the morgue. But I suppose you missed all that."

"We must have gotten away just in time. But now that you mention it, I did hear something as we drove away. Like a truck backfiring. Something like that."

"Cute," Ed said. "At least two shotguns and something else, maybe a big bore handgun, and you *think* you heard a *truck*?"

"Well, it sounded like a big truck."

"I bet it did."

"So who were they?" I said.

Ricco said, "One of them was a scumbag—pardon my French, ma'am—named Willard Rumbitt. We don't know about the other one yet. He didn't have no ID on him."

I said, "Gang fight, probably."

"Naw," Ricco said. "The John Doe was four, five blocks away with his gu—Uh, he couldn't have made it that far with his belly missing."

"Rumbitt," Marge said. "Rumbitt, Rumbitt. Why, that name sounds almost like a frog, doesn't it?"

Ed and Ricco stared at her. I smiled and kicked her under the table. George looked nervous.

Ed stroked his wobbly chin. "Maybe we should talk to the Rosencrantz woman," he said. "Maybe she saw something."

"Don't see how, Ed," I said. "She was with me."

"Where is she now?"

"That's hard to say. I'm sure she's safe enough. Of course, if there was a formal charge or an official request, I might be able to find her and convince her to talk to you. With her lawyer present, naturally."

Ed gave me a long look, then he said, "No, not yet, anyway. I'll let you know."

Ricco looked surprised, but then Ricco would have pushed it to avoid the appearance of backing down. Little guys tend to be funny that way.

"Seen Cowboy lately?" Ed asked.

"Been a fair while," I said. "Last I heard, he had a horse ranch—or whatever you call it—out toward Denton."

"He's still there. You know, there were two pickups stolen last night, too."

"Only two? Must have been a slow night."

"Only two I'm interested in," Ed said. "One of them wrecked three motorcycles parked across from the Dew Drop Inn."

"Kids," I said. "Probably couldn't reach the brake pedal."

"And the other one was dumped in Grand Prairie."

"Grand Prairie's a long way from the Dew Drop Inn. If you're trying to make a connection."

"I know where Grand Prairie is. It's not all that far. And one of the Dew Drop girls says the same make and color pickup was parked out front last night."

"Lots of pickups on the road, Ed. Pick one, you'll find another one just like it somewhere."

"Yeah, that's true," Ed said. He slurped his coffee. "Cowboy always liked pickups."

"*All* cowboys like pickups. They've replaced the horse, I hear. Come-a-ti-yi-yippy-yippy-ay. The Marlboro man double-clutches."

Ed heaved himself up. "Wish I could spend the day playing word games with you, Rafferty. Some of us have to work." Ricco stood up, too, and looked longingly at the tennis court and swimming pool.

Marge showed them out. George went along a few steps behind. He brushed the edge of the sliding glass door with his shoulder and jumped nervously.

I waited at the table. With any luck, Consuela might come out and smile at me.

Marge and George didn't return for a long time. When they did, George was flushed and stubborn. Marge looked angry.

"George wants to fire you," she said to me. She ignited another Virginia Slim and stood hipshot, with her right elbow resting on her left fist. "Go on, George. Tell him why."

"I just don't think . . . Well, it won't do Vivian any good, and with people dying, maybe—"

"You'd shoot a rabid dog, wouldn't you?" Marge said. There was contempt in her voice.

"Don't tell me," I said. "Let me guess. That's either Margaret Thatcher, Indira Gandhi, or Lady Macbeth, I'm not sure which."

Marge huffed at me. She was a world-class huffer.

"George," I said, "let me save you the trouble of asking. No. You're too late. I can't stop now."

"But—"

"But nothing. It's true none of this will do Vivian any good. You should have known that from the first. What do you think, we can say King's X and walk away? The bikers are stirred up now. I can't quit and spend the next year looking over my shoulder because you lost your nerve, for Christ's sake! I have a lady to protect—"

"Well," Marge said, "I hardly think this motorcycle slut is—"

"Not Fran. *My* lady. Turk and his pals know about me. They might try me when Hilda's around. I won't risk that. You can quit, I suppose. But I can't."

George flapped his arms in frustration and went to stand at the other end of the patio.

Marge laughed bitterly. "My God, how incredibly chivalrous. I suppose I don't need to pay you now, since you intend to do the work anyway."

"Somehow I don't think that's a serious suggestion, Marge. I think I'm just handy and a better target than your husband right now. But okay, let's say you fire me. The question is, what would I do, right?"

I held up a finger for point one. "I'd forget about getting legal evidence. Instead, I'd concentrate on driving them away. Maybe I could convince them the stakes are too high. Maybe I'd have to kill them."

I found another finger and showed it to her. "Second—if you decide not to pay, you would never know how it turns out. Your blood lust would simmer unslaked. How's that for a turn of phrase?"

I raised a third finger, but couldn't think of anything it stood for. I finally said, "And I'd take you off my Christmas card list. That would fix you."

"You have a mouth like a snotty kid, Rafferty." Marge sighed and rubbed her forehead with the back of her hand. "You're not fired. Go back to work."

"You'll pay an extra nine grand just to hear the gory details? You have expensive tastes."

"You're not expensive, Rafferty. In my position, wouldn't you give two weeks' pay to know when this nightmare was over?"

Put that way, she had a good point.

CHAPTER SEVENTEEN

Rafferty's Rule Six says: Don't forget the money.

I went to Dermott's office for my six thousand dollars. Marge had phoned him, so the check was ready when I scaled the heights of Bryan Tower. Dermott looked at the check on his desk, looked at me, and said, "Should I ask how you earned this, Rafferty?"

"You're an officer of the court, right? Bound by the ethics of the bar association, sworn to defend justice, fair play, motherhood, apple pie, and Sunday school. Upon sober reflection, Counselor, I don't think you want to know how I earned that."

He signed the check and I left him to the sanitary practice of law. Devising tax shelters, beating DWI raps, leasing deductible Mercedes; clean-cut honest work like that.

I split the six grand into two parts. Enough for the final payment on the Mustang and two month's house rent went into my checking account. I bought a six-month CD with the rest; it made me feel like a budding tycoon.

Move over, Mollison. And, by the way, where do you find maids like Consuela?

The noontime shadow-boxing with Ed Durkee had left a thought dangling. I went to see if I could tie a knot in the end of it and use it to reel in Turk and his band of merry men.

* * *

The Dew Drop Inn looked even shabbier in the daytime. Without the blurred edges of night, it was only a tacky white building surrounded by patched asphalt. Across the street, where Mimi had flattened the motorcycles, the curb was empty.

The hot Ford pickup was sure to be in the police impound yard. Were the motorcycles there, too?

I walked around trying to look like I was detecting something and found that the stretch of curb wasn't *quite* empty. There was a bright red plastic shard there, and a section of amber turn signal, and a dusting of headlight fragments. Rockford or Magnum or Mike Hammer would have been able to glance at the debris, say "Ah-ha!" and rattle off the motorcycle model, license number, mileage since the last oil change, and the shoe size of the rider.

To me, it was just broken plastic and glass.

Everything's easier on television.

The guy who ran the police impound yard was a civilian. He'd been around. He wasn't impressed by real cops; private types like me bored him rigid.

He had a shack outside the wire mesh fence. Inside the shack, he had a file cabinet, a chair, two *Hustler* centerfolds showing everything but the G-spot, and a shelf with a radio on it. A loud radio.

What with the radio and a dead cigar stub in the corner of his mouth, he was hard to understand. He made up for that by saying only one thing. "You don't have no release, you don't get no car."

"Not a car, dammit. I told you already. Three motorcycles. Watch my lips—mo-tor-cy-cles. Look there, you've got me doing Dom DeLuise imitations, for God's sake!"

"You don't have no release, you don't get no car."

"Hey, it's only a lousy insurance case. Three bikes. They would have come late last night, early this morning."

The soggy cigar shifted briefly to the center of his mouth,

then darted back to the corner. I smiled at him and tried to look trustworthy and deserving. "I only want to *see* them. Just for a second."

"You don't have no release, you don't—"

"Fifty bucks for two minutes with the bikes."

"Do I look like I work Vice? Get outta here!"

"I think I understand now," I said. "I don't get no car."

"Jeez, it took you long enough."

I went home then and carefully went through my house. I had the cocked .45 in my fist. Even so, I caught myself tiptoeing around like a dowager wondering when that pesky mouse was going to run over her foot. There were no bikers hiding in closets or under the bed; nothing ticked or exploded. If Turk et al knew where I lived, they had done nothing except, perhaps, drive past and look.

Actually, it was a trifle disappointing.

I phoned Hilda, caught her at the shop and suggested a night on the town.

"Okay," she said. "I'm ready for that." She sounded preoccupied. "What do you have in mind?"

"Drinks, dinner, and play it by ear from there?"

"Sure."

"Hil, do you mind if we take Fran, too?"

"What, now I have a kid sister? Be a sport, Rafferty, give her a quarter. Maybe she'll go to the candy store and leave us alone."

"If you really don't want her, that's okay. I just thought it would be a way for you two to get acquainted on neutral territory."

Hilda sighed. "No, it's okay. She can come along, I guess."

When I dialed Hilda's number, the phone rang for a long time before Fran answered. "Hi," I said, "did I catch you in the shower?"

"I wish you had. I'm cleaning the oven. I've got yucky

brown foam all over my hands. If we get cut off, it'll be because the phone melted.''

"Good girl," I said. "Fran, it's Friday night and time to party. I'll pick you girls up about seven-thirty.''

"Oh, great!" she said. "Uh, have you talked to Hilda yet?''

"Sure. She's looking forward to it.''

"I hope so. This morning was kind of . . . oh, I don't know. Weird, I guess.''

"I wouldn't say weird, Fran. I thought it was funny. You two were so busy walking around each other saying 'excuse me' and 'pardon me' and 'after you,' it sounded like an etiquette class.''

She giggled. "It was tense, wasn't it? It's your fault, though, for pushing Hilda into letting me stay here. She's awfully good to you.''

"She's the best there is, Fran. I'll see you later.''

"Hey, wait a minute! Where are we going tonight? What am I going to wear?''

"Talk to Hilda when she gets home. She'll have an idea.''

"Rafferty!" she wailed.

"Bye, Fran.''

Women have the damnedest problems.

I made coffee, lit a pipe, and cleaned the .45. If the Colt had been registered, I might have worried about whether the cops had recovered the slug that went through Frog.

Instead, I wondered how to handle Turk, Stomper, and Smokey Joe. There seemed to be two possible ways to approach the problem. I could wait for them to find me, drag any survivors to the cops, and hope Fran's testimony—and a confession?—would be enough to convict. Or I could find them first, drag any survivors to the cops, et cetera, et cetera.

Going after the bikers was probably the cleanest way to wrap up the Mollison case. It would get Fran out of Hilda's hair faster, keep the bikers off-balance, and maybe keep any bystanders from ending up like Joe Zifretti.

And, in accordance with Rule Six, it would put another nine grand in my bank account.

There was also the off-chance they would run, not fight. That would be the most peaceful solution. It was open-ended, though, and unsatisfying. It would cost me money, for one thing. For another, I was like Marge Mollison. I wanted to know when it was over.

I reassembled the Colt, dry-fired it, reloaded it, put it down, and smiled at it. I always liked that big ungainly cannon. The army has replaced it now with a wimpy little 9mm Beretta. Dumb.

I checked in with the answering service. Surprise, surprise, there were calls to return. I had forgotten about my biker-bashing newspaper ads. Not that they had been needed. Since Turk and his followers had surfaced in Dallas, I didn't expect much from the half a dozen country people who left messages. I noted the numbers anyway, looked at the list for a minute, then said the hell with it. It was Friday evening and I liked the sound of a weekend off.

I watched bits and pieces of the news while I showered and changed. The Bobbsey Twins at Newsroom Corner ooh-ed and aah-ed over the Dew Drop shooting. They called it a gang fight, read corny jokes off the auto-cue, and chuckled their way into a commercial break. During the first commercial, a car dealer with big teeth promised me his salesmen were the easiest pushovers in Dallas. He dragged a salesman on screen to prove it. Guy looked like a grave robber to me.

I put on dark blue slacks, a new pale yellow shirt and a lightweight sports coat. The ensemble also included a stylish shoulder holster and a .38; I decided it made more sense to not need it than to not have it.

I went out the door with my chest stuck out, feeling clean and tough and ready for anything. Wearing a shoulder holster does that to you for the first few minutes.

Hilda answered her door wearing a flimsy yellow summer dress with a black belt that picked up the dark secrets of her eyes and hair. She smiled and said, "Come on in. This may take a while. She's dressing."

"You two getting along all right?"

"Well enough. She's trying, no doubt about that. The kitchen is spotless. I'm just not used to coming home and having anyone here."

"I'm here sometimes."

She puckered up for a kiss. "That's different." She screwed a fingernail into my ribs. "How you doing, big guy?"

"Tolerable, ma'am, tolerable. Especially now that I got me a date with the new schoolmarm."

Hilda backed away with a wry smile. "Well, don't forget Miss Kitty. She's coming, too."

We sat on the couch and held hands. Hilda told me she was working on a job for Fran. She might know something definite on Monday. I thanked her. She said her monumental effort was a direct result of my surprise incentive program. I patted her thigh and said, "There, there."

"Wrong," said Hilda. "It's not there-there at all. And if you don't finish this case in a week as promised, you'll never see where-where it is again."

"Now that's what I call an incentive program."

Fran came into the living room. She had the shy eagerness of a young girl ready for the junior prom. She wore a tan shift with big buttons down the front. It was a touch casual, perhaps, but she made up for it with excitement.

I liked that Fran even more than the hausfrau model. And it was hard to imagine her half-naked, hustling the Dew Drop Inners for watered drinks.

Hilda's BMW was better suited for the occasion than my weary Mustang, so we drove to the Hyatt Regency with Teutonic efficiency.

During the meal, Fran watched Hilda before she selected a fork or decided which bread plate to use. I wondered how many times she had eaten anywhere more uptown than a Denny's or McDonald's.

I ordered Caesar salad. The waiter assembled it on a cart at tableside, which fascinated Fran. "Hey," she said, "imagine having a salad made right here, especially for you."

"Ah, stand by for dessert."

We had Bananas Foster, Crepes Suzette, and Cherries Jubilee, *flambéd* simultaneously on three different carts. It cost me twenty bucks in tips and our corner of the room looked like the burning of Atlanta.

Fran loved it. So did the waiters; they discreetly leered at Fran's chest between abracadabra moves with brandy bottles and matches.

After the meal, we strolled across to Reunion Tower for afterdinner drinks. When the high-speed elevator did its "we have liftoff" number, Hilda swayed against me and I put my arm around her. She noticed the shoulder holster and flipped my coat open. "Did you have to wear that thing?"

Fran had been watching the numbers light up over the elevator door. She turned and said, "Excuse me?"

Hilda tugged open my coat again and jerked her thumb at the shoulder holster. "The big guy brought his substitute penis."

Fran goggled at Hilda and me; she looked shocked.

Hilda said, "No, wait a minute. That's just a figure of speech." She babbled something about Freud and male macho psychology; Fran got it almost immediately and began to giggle.

"What a dummy," she said. "I thought you meant . . . ."

The pair of them were whooping and wiping their eyes when the elevator stopped and the door swooshed open. A middle-aged couple in evening dress frowned and stood aside while we stepped out.

"I caught these kids playing with the elevator," I said. "Call the cops, will you?"

"Call two cops," Hilda chortled. "And we will not accept substitutes."

Fran turned red and chewed on her hand.

The fancy-dress couple ignored us, entered the elevator, and studied the overhead light until the door closed. They were very interested in that light.

A slim black girl in a long red dress led us around to a table on the outer rim, next to the tall windows. We sat in soft comfortable chairs and ordered drinks. Irish coffee for Hilda; a moment's hesitation, then the same for Fran. Scotch for me.

When the hostess turned away, Fran soberly studied the circular room and said, "Pretty high caliber place, eh?" The girls broke up again.

Somewhere, Emily Post whirled in her grave.

After they settled down, Hilda and Fran soaked up the view. They stared out at the city revolving below us and pointed out places to each other. Fran thought just maybe she could see where her apartment was.

Dallas is a pretty city at night and Reunion Tower is high enough to let you see all of it. I watched the lights, and the dark patches, too, and wondered where out there the bikers were hiding.

We drove back to Hilda's long after midnight, content and a little boozy. Fran dozed in the back seat.

Half a block from the house, I saw a figure standing on the dark sidewalk. I nosed the BMW into the curb and flicked on the high beams. It was a tall thin man in gray trousers and a white shirt. He shielded his eyes with one hand and called softly. I couldn't hear what he said. Then a fat black Labrador came tail-wagging out of the bushes. The man and his dog hurried away.

Feeling foolish, I backed clear of the curb and drove four doors down to Hilda's.

Inside, Fran stepped out of her shoes and went dreamily toward her bedroom, holding her shoes with two fingers hooked through the straps. "Night," she said. "Thank you very much."

I drank a glass of milk in the kitchen and watched Hilda pull off her earrings and scratch her head sleepily. "Did you have a good time?"

"Yes," she said. "And now I feel guilty about that kid sister crack. She's all right, isn't she? She tries so hard. Did you see how careful she was at dinner?"

"She spent a long time on the back of a bike, Hil.

She's going to make it, though. She wants to. That's important.''

"You might be right. Come on, let's go to bed. Rub my back?''

I rubbed her back, then we fell asleep nestled together like two spoons.

CHAPTER EIGHTEEN

Saturday morning. I mowed Hilda's lawn. When I stopped to refuel the mower, Fran brought me a beer.

"Here," she said. "You look hot."

"Sweating off that meal last night. Thanks."

She sat cross-legged on the lawn and squinted up at me. "Can you drive me to my place this afternoon? I forgot a few things in the rush."

"Sure. I may have to go out anyway. Let me make a call first, then we'll pick a time."

"Okay, thanks," said Fran. "Maybe Hilda would like to come, too."

"No, she'll stay here. I don't think there will be any trouble, but it's not Hilda's fight."

"Oh." She looked down.

"Don't get uptight and read too much into that," I said to the top of her head.

She nodded and tugged at a hand-sized patch of crabgrass. "You two aren't married, right?"

"No."

"Are you going to?"

"Get married?" I said. "I don't think so."

"Why not?"

"It doesn't seem necessary. Being married didn't help you and Tony much, did it?"

She shook her head.

"It's the people that count, not the paperwork, Fran."

"Sure," she said.

She fiddled with the crabgrass. I drank my beer. Finally, she looked up at me and said, "What made you feel you had to help me get away from the bikers the other night?"

"I hereby invoke the streaker's defense. It seemed a good idea at the time. Besides, there was nothing good on the tube, so . . ."

"Not good enough," Fran said. "You're joking because you're embarrassed."

"Me? The man who once mooned a presidential press conference? No way!"

"You never did that."

"Well," I said, "it was on Channel Eight at the time. Did I forget to mention that?"

Fran said, "You joke, and recite those silly rules, too, but you feel strongly about obligations and honor and things, don't you?"

I drained the beer and crushed the can. And remembered my teenage days, when crushing a beer can with one hand required a little work. They must make them out of tinfoil today.

"Okay, Fran," I said. "You got me. I am embarrassed. A little. Because you're getting into ethics and feelings and why I do things. Stuff like that. And it's hard to talk about such things without sounding like a pompous jerk."

"Try. Please."

"You were in a tight spot. I put you there by asking questions and poking around. So I had to get you out. I owed you."

"I don't know anybody else who would have thought that," she said.

"I don't know anybody else who has to look me in the eye when I shave."

"It's not that simple," said Fran.

"No, probably not," I said. "But that's all you're entitled to for one lousy beer. Now get lost, woman. I have a lawn to mow."

"Yessir!" She got up, brushed off her bottom. "Let me know what time we're going, huh?"

After I finished the lawn, I phoned the cop shop. Ed Durkee was off for the day; Ricco was due in at four.

Fran and I went to her apartment; there was no one around. I wasn't exactly disappointed, but I did wonder why Turk and his buddies had been so quiet for the past two days.

Back at Hilda's, after lunch, I took a nap on the couch. I woke up an hour later to see Hilda and Fran across the room whispering about an old oil lamp on a corner table. It was a handsome lamp, converted to electricity in the twenties or thirties, according to Hilda, and it had a big green glass shade I liked. They looked at it and whispered, flipped pages in a soft cover antique book, and whispered some more.

Hilda saw me looking at them. "Oops," she said. "Sorry. Go back to sleep."

They left with the book, still whispering. I went back to sleep. When I work at it, I do great naps.

At four-thirty, I phoned Ricco. "You," he said. "After dumping that bullshit on me and Ed yesterday, now you want a favor?"

"Some favor, Ricco. What's the big deal about the motorcycles from the Dew Drop?"

"I don't know what the big deal is. You're the one who's asking."

"You're the one who put me onto Fran Rosencrantz and the Dew Drop," I said. "It occurred to me if bikers shot up the neighborhood, maybe they're connected to the Mollison snatch."

"Yeah, and maybe them old farts in Washington are gonna repeal *Miranda*. Hold your breath."

"Come on, Ricco. What happened to the bikes?"

"How the hell do I know?"

I tried patience and reason. "Look in the file. You're up to your ears in paper down there; someone must have written it down."

"The file, smart-ass, is in Ed's desk. In case you don't

remember, certain people here get uptight when they catch certain other people messing around in a lieutenant's desk without his say-so.''

"Call Ed, then.''

"Oh, sure. Call Ed, he says. What's Ed got to do on a Saturday off? He'd love to be bothered at home because you got some wild-ass idea. All right, look, Rafferty, leave it with me, okay? Where are you? I'll call you back.''

Twenty minutes later, he was on the phone again. "You owe me for all this trouble, Rafferty. Remember that.''

"Hot damn, this must be a biggie. Wait, let me sit down.''

"Go on, fuck around,'' he said. "It won't do you no good. I don't know what happened to the motorcycles.'' He pronounced the word *motor-sickles*. "Maybe they're in the impound yard; maybe they already been claimed. If they wasn't banged up too bad, maybe the owners rode 'em away that night. I don't know. All I got here is the original squeal. A uniformed squad worked the traffic part of it. LaFranchi and Hooten. Talk to them.''

"Hell, Ricco, you must have their report.''

"Maybe. It could be in the lieutenant's office with the rest of the crap or it might be in the patrol office waiting for a clerk to file it in the wrong place. Get off my back, Rafferty. Ask LaFranchi or Hooten. That's the best I can do for you.''

"Okay, thanks. Uh, you got a number for either of them?''

"Jesus,'' Ricco said. "Hang on.'' The phone went dead for six minutes.

When Ricco came back, he said, "LaFranchi started his vacation today. Hooten's off, working the evening shift tomorrow. And I can't fart around with you all day. I gotta go look at a nigger stiff in a South Dallas shooting gallery. Fuck off, Rafferty.'' The phone went dead again and stayed that way.

* * *

That night, I took Hilda and Fran to hear the Dallas Jazz Orchestra in a bar off Greenville Avenue.

Some people worry about whales; me, I'd rather keep the big bands alive. If they made Glenn Miller T-shirts, I'd wear one.

Among other things, the DJO played ''MacArthur Park,'' their long arrangement, with a searing trumpet solo that made the hair on my arms stand up. It was fantastic.

During a break, Fran said they weren't Fleetwood Mac, but they were ''kind of nice.''

Hilda patted my hand and said, ''Don't scowl like that, Rafferty. Look at it this way. You're not Tom Selleck, but you're kind of nice, too.''

It was that kind of a Saturday night. I wondered why I bothered to take them anywhere.

CHAPTER NINETEEN

Sunday was a hot, bright day. The sun had a searing, angry look it usually didn't get until later in the summer. It was a good day for loafing indoors. With the air-conditioner on high.

We lazed around with the papers, then fixed brunch. Fran had never tried Eggs Benedict before; she said she liked them, but they seemed a lot of trouble to make.

Around noon, Hilda and Fran went through another antique lesson. Then they wandered into the living room and Hilda looked around with a let's-rearrange-the-furniture expression on her face.

I jumped up, kissed her hard, patted her on the backside, and suggested we go for a drive. It worked.

We took Hilda's car again, mainly because her air-conditioner worked. After tooling around aimlessly for a half an hour, I drove to White Rock Lake and stopped.

The girls laughed. From the backseat, Fran said, "You were right. I owe you a dollar."

"Cheeky wenches," I said. "What's that all about?"

Fran said, "Hilda bet we would end up here. She says you're a freak for sailboats."

"I just like to look at them, that's all."

There was a dinghy race underway. The leaders rounded

an orange marker buoy and three gaudy spinnakers went up, one after another.

"Ooh," Fran said. "Pretty."

"You see," I said to Hilda, "some people have good taste."

"Don't get him started, Fran," Hilda said. "He pretends he knows that sailing jargon. He becomes insufferable."

"Go on, Rafferty," said Fran. "Talk me some sailing."

"The fleet has rounded the weather mark," I said. "They've hoisted spinnakers and are running with the wind over the starboard quarter. Spindle-sheet the grundle board. Winch in the genoa sheet. Ketch cutter sloop schooner."

"Does that make sense?"

"Not all of it," I said. "But doesn't it sound terrific?"

Fran peered at the dinghies rushing over the lake. "You couldn't take one of those boats out into the ocean, could you?"

"No. Too small. And they're open boats. Although people have sailed around the world in boats that weren't much larger."

"Wow," Fran said. "That would be scary."

"Yeah," I said. "What a kick!"

"Come on, Walter Mitty," said Hilda. "Pretend you're a big spender. Buy us an ice cream cone."

"You want me to stop looking at boats and chase around after *ice cream*?"

"Yep," Hilda said. "And I want real ice cream, not that machine junk. Two scoops."

"Okay," I said, "but you better come across tonight, baby, or I'll tell all the guys you're just a tease."

We walked slowly along the shore, racing the heat for the drippy cones. I walked behind the girls, both of whom wore shorts. I even found time to watch the boats occasionally.

"I appreciate what you've done for me, Hilda," Fran said.

"Thank Rafferty," said Hilda. "He has a thing about people in trouble. He has to right every wrong, like a kid."

She laughed. "Can't you just imagine him when he was little, with a black eye and a slingshot and a stray puppy?"

"I'm serious. Okay, lending me a room for a day or two is one thing, but you've been extra . . . friendly. And understanding." Fran twirled her chocolate cone against her tongue. "Do you really think you can help me find a job?"

Hilda chased a strawberry rivulet down her hand. "Ummm. Let you know tomorrow night, I hope."

"Great. Thanks again. Oh, damn!" Fran dabbed at her sticky fingers with a tissue.

"You two are sloppy as hell," I said. "Look at me. Finished the ice cream cone. Still clean and neat. Rule Sixteen: Don't get any on you."

"Ignore him," said Hilda. "He stopped back there to wash his hands in the lake."

I didn't think she'd seen that.

The girls and I split up at 3:30. They went to prowl the antique shops that stayed open on Sundays. I went looking for Patrolman Hooten.

I expected Hooten to be a cornfed bull-rider type. Don't ask me why; even trained supersleuths can jump to conclusions.

Patrolman Hooten turned out to be Patrolwoman Hooten. She was, I judged, a quarter-inch over the department's minimum height requirement. How she made the weight was anyone's guess; I've heard of people gorging on bananas and milkshakes.

Louise Hooten had fine sandy hair cut in the style we used to call Duck's Ass in my misspent youth. She had a narrow face with a marginally oversized nose, pale blue eyes, teeth that had never seen braces, and a uniform so immaculate she could have been trained in only one place.

"Let me guess," I said. "Marines?"

Hooten nodded. "They wouldn't let me go to Lebanon," she said, "so I didn't re-up. Hey, the sergeant said you'd be looking for me. Make it quick, will you? We're due on patrol."

Behind her, a muscular officer started to slide behind the wheel of a squad car. He looked at Hooten's back, shrugged, and walked around to the passenger side.

I said, "Thursday night, you and LaFranchi worked a hit-and-run at a beer joint off Industrial. A pickup creamed three motorcycles. I'm trying to find the owners of those bikes."

She folded her arms. Her leather equipment belt cracked. "What's your interest?"

"Last year, five bikers kidnapped a college girl. Drugged her, hauled her around for nine, ten months, then dumped her. Those three bikes may belong to the group."

"I heard about that," she said. "How is she?"

I shook my head and tapped my temple.

"Pricks," said Hooten.

"I can get the information from Homicide, probably," I said, "except the grunts on the line usually know what really happened, don't they?"

Okay, "grunts on the line" was hokey. So what? Sometimes you play to the audience.

Hooten said, "I can't tell you much. Once they got the pickup off those bikes, they weren't hurt too badly. Owners took them away."

"Didn't Homicide want to talk to the riders?"

"The owners told us they had been inside having a beer when it happened," Hooten said. "It was a fender-bender. No injuries. We had no reason to hold the victims, for Chrissake. Dino gave 'em accident report forms. For the insurance, you know."

"With a shooting across the street, I'm surprised Homicide wasn't more interested."

"Yeah, well, I think Dino and I might hear about that." She said it with the resigned indifference of the low-ranking professional.

"You must have filed a report, though," I said. "You did take the plate numbers of the bikes?"

"Oh, sure," she said. She tugged a notebook from her hip pocket, flipped pages, and read out three license numbers. "You got a way to run these?"

"I can bum a favor from somebody," I said.

"Naw," she said, "don't bother. I'll slide them in with our routine plate checks tonight. Where can I reach you?"

I wrote Hilda's number on the back of a card and gave it to her. She read it, nodded, and said, "You the one who wasted the other two bikers?"

I spread my hands and raised my eyebrows. "Me? Look at this face. I ask you, would I do that?"

"I would," Hooten said. "I'd waste those suckers in a minute, if they gave me a halfway decent excuse."

Memo to motorcycle gang PR men: definite image problems with women in the 18-to-30 age group.

I went to the office, wrote checks for the more urgent bills, then met Hilda and Fran as planned. We went to Denny's for supper. Hilda told Fran I would kill for a Denny's patty melt. I denied that and ate three while they nudged each other and laughed.

We were back at Hilda's watching a *M*A*S*H* rerun— an old, old one, with Trapper and Frank and Henry Blake— when Hooten called with the bad news.

"We both got troubles, Rafferty," she said. "Those bikes were Harleys. I'd swear to that. But the computer says the plates came off two Hondas and a Yamaha from Dalton County."

CHAPTER TWENTY

Cowboy and I pulled into Conover at four o'clock the next afternoon. I shook him awake when I stopped at a red light. He took his hat off his face, yawned, and said, "Looks like a purty little town."

"Population two thousand six hundred forty-two," I said. "Rotary Club meets on Wednesday, Lions on Tuesday. Drive Carefully, We Love Our Children. And the Exxon station has a special on batteries."

Conover was three hours from Dallas, out I-30 to Mount Pleasant, then down Texas 49 and 11. It was thirteen miles from Daingerfield, just over the Dalton County line and near the eastern edge of the State Park. The surrounding countryside was pretty; hilly, green, and forested, especially in the park.

Texas 11 went straight through Conover. In passing, it formed one side of the courthouse square. At least it looked like a courthouse square, even though Conover was not a county seat. Maybe it used to be; maybe they planned to bid for it.

The "courthouse" was a muddy-red stone blockhouse centered in a yellowing lawn. The building looked closed; a sign on the main entrance said something about the Dalton County Historical Society. I couldn't read the rest of it. There was a black WWI artillery piece in the southeast corner of the square and tired shade trees between the side-walk and the street.

I turned left and started around the square.

There were benches under the trees on the courthouse side and stores with metal awnings on the other side. We passed the hardware store, the bank, a furniture place, a drugstore, and the Odeon Theater, which had a weekends-only look about it. There was also a gift shop, cafe, small-appliance store, video rental place, and another drugstore/magazine stand/soda fountain/you name it. People on the sidewalk stopped and turned and watched us cruise slowly past. Conover was a small town, all right.

"Don't see no sign that says This Way to the Bad Guys," Cowboy said.

"If it was that easy, I wouldn't be paying you two-fifty a day."

"I know'd there was a reason," he said.

I turned down a street leading away from the square. There was a Goodyear dealer in the first block, then three blocks of small frame houses, then we were back in the country. I went back to the square and tried another street. Almost identical.

"Wonder where William J. Dolan hangs out," I said.

"Pull in over there," said Cowboy. "Let's find out."

"Over there" was in front of a streetside bench where two old men sat. Cowboy got out, stretched, and leaned against the Mustang. He shoved his hands into his jeans pockets, looked everywhere except directly at the old-tim-ers, and said, "Howdy."

One said, "Ha-doo." The other nodded.

"Looking for Billy Dolan," Cowboy said. "Be grateful if you could hep me."

"Seen you go past before," one of the men said. "You a friend of Billy's?"

"Not so's you'd notice," said Cowboy. "Friend ast me to look him up, I was ever out this way." Cowboy's drawl had thickened.

The old men nodded, then one spat in the dusty grass,

and said, "He works for his daddy. Ford place on the highway. He rides one of them scooters."

"Much obliged."

"Damfool things, them scooters. Ain't even Amerkin."

The other ancient cackled. "Member when Dusty got him a franchise fer them leetle Jap cars? Went bust in six months. Can't sell stuff made right here in the U S of A, don't sell nothing, I say."

Cowboy got into the Mustang. He touched a finger to his big hat. "Thank ya kindly, gentlemen."

In the rearview mirror, I saw them watch us pull away, then stick their heads together secretively.

I hadn't noticed a Ford place on the way into town, so we headed east from the square.

Dolan Ford was a half mile out of town, across the highway from the Conover Cafe and Drive-in. There were more tractors on display than cars. There was a gas pump at one corner of the gray-painted building, so I let a lanky teenager in a Ford cap fill the tank.

"You Billy Dolan?"

He pointed around the building. "Inna back. That'll be $16.93."

The rear half of the building was a cavernous workshop. It was cluttered, dim, and relatively cool. There was no one there except Billy Dolan, who wore once-white coveralls unzipped to the waist. He polished the speed fairing on a metallic-red Honda and listened intently.

"Sheriff's office over at Dalton said you reported your license plate stolen Friday."

"Right," he said. "Sure would like to catch whoever took it." Billy was nineteen, maybe twenty, with shaggy red hair and a round, open face.

"When and where was it taken, Billy?"

"You're not from the sheriff's office, are you?"

I showed him my license. That was worth taking a break from the wax job. "Hot damn," he said. "A private eye! Ain't that something!"

"It's a dirty job, but someone has to do it."

"Man, I'd do it! You bet I would."

He didn't know he was being teased and I was sorry I'd said it. "Billy, I'm working on a case that might be related to your stolen plate. I'd appreciate it if you could help me."

"Sure! Hell, yes. Whatcha want to know?"

"When was the plate taken?"

"Wish I knew," he said. "See, I didn't notice it was gone till Bubba Smith told me somebody took the plate off'n his Yammer. R. L. lost his, too. They gone over to see the sheriff today."

"When did this Bubba Smith realize his plate was missing?"

"Friday morning," Billy said. "But he don't know when it was took."

"You hang around with Bubba and R. L. much?"

"Hell, yes. We went to school together."

"Well, when was the last time you're certain the plate was still on your bike?"

He frowned and thought. "It must have been there last Tuesday. 'Cause I washed the bike, see, and I think I'd have missed the plate if it was gone then."

"Okay, that helps. Sometime between Tuesday and Friday morning, let's say. Could your buddies' plates have been taken the same time as yours?"

"Could be. We was all out drinkin' beer Wednesday night. Maybe they was took then." He grinned proudly. "I mean to tell ya, we sure couldn't see much after closing time. No way!"

Cowboy stood in the background, leaning against a huge tractor with tires higher than his hat.

"Billy," I said, "the plates stolen from you and your friends showed up in Dallas on three Harleys. Outlaw bikers."

I suddenly realized I hadn't thought about the plates on the bikes owned by Becker and Frog. "Uh, Billy, have you heard about any other plates stolen around here?"

"No. Just Bubba, R. L., and me. 'Course, there's lotsa bikes in the county and I don't know everybody."

"That's another thing. Any outlaw bikers live around here?"

"Don't think so. I mean, hell's bells, you see outlaws passing through every once in a while. That's all." He grinned at me. "You know how it is, though. Them outlaws are like niggers; they all look alike."

"Okay. Where is this bar where the plates were taken?"

" 'Bout halfway between here and Hughes Springs," he said. "Now, I don't know for sure that's when it happened, mind. Probably, though." He nodded his big head a few times. By the time he finished, he sounded positive. "Musta been then."

"Thanks, Billy." I pointed at his bike. "Is that color Candy Apple Red?"

"Just red, far as I know. Why?"

"When I was a kid," I said, "Candy Apple Red was *the* color. Every hot-rod had to be Candy Apple Red. It was like a requirement."

Billy Dolan shrugged. "Never heard of it."

Cowboy levered himself away from the tractor and said, "Come on, old-timer. This ain't no trivia game."

We left Billy Dolan to his polishing.

"I feel like an idiot," I said to Cowboy. I told him about forgetting the other two bikes. "The one Mimi shot might have had stolen plates. And I bet the one I got had a bike stashed behind the Dew Drop. If those plates were hot, too, we'd have a better idea where their base is."

"My, my," Cowboy said. "This investigation stuff is complicated, ain't it? Glad I don't have a license for it. Too much responsibility."

"Shut up, Cowboy."

"That's no way to talk to hired help, Rafferty. Don't you know nothing about industrial relations?"

We stood by the side of the highway, watching the light traffic, squinting in the sun. I wondered what to do first. For a change, there seemed to be a variety of choices.

We could go back to Dalton and check for additional reports of missing motorcycle plates. We could look up Billy's friends Bubba and R. L. We could get a motel room—if there was a motel in Conover—and answer the phone calls I had received from the newspaper ads. At the same time, I could call Ed Durkee about the other two bikes.

Or we could stand by the roadside, watch dusty pickups and lost tourists go by, and hope something good fell in our laps.

And that's what happened.

Rafferty's Rule Thirty-four: Sometimes good luck accomplishes more than hard work.

"Well, don't that beat all!" Cowboy said, staring across the two-lane highway at the tacky drive-in opposite. I looked, too, and saw the black Harley at the same time the rider spotted us.

He had pulled off the road onto the gravel drive-in lot before he saw us. When he gunned the bike, he nearly lost it. The rear end slewed one way, then the other. A rooster-tail of stones and dust sprayed head-high. Then the bike hit the road surface again and it jerked violently upright. I thought it would go over onto its side.

Good luck only runs so far, though. The biker saved it at the last minute. He did a tight U-turn in front of a Chevy with a roof rack and roared back the way he had come, headed away from Conover.

Cowboy and I were on the move by then, too, and we were fast enough to cut off the same Chevy. It had out-of-state plates, and it stopped dead, probably wishing it was back where it came from, where people didn't drive like these crazy Texans.

I pushed the reluctant Mustang up through the gears while Cowboy knelt on his seat and rummaged through his soft sports-bag on the backseat. "How 'bout that, Rafferty?" he said. "We in business, after all!"

"You recognize him?" I shouted. The windows were open and it was noisy as hell at seventy-five. Two hundred yards ahead, the bike still pulled away slightly.

"Uumph," Cowboy grunted as we bottomed out in a dip in the road. "Hairy one on the left of that skinhead dude.'' He poked my right thigh with something. ''Don't drop that,'' he yelled.

When I found an instant to look down, there was a Ruger Blackhawk wedged under my leg.

At ninety, the Mustang reminded me how badly it needed a front end alignment. The steering wheel bucked and jerked nervously. I kept my foot on the floor anyway. The bike was still two hundred yards ahead, but we were holding that position.

Cowboy turned around and dropped into his seat. His arms were full of shotgun pieces. ''Rough ridin'est goddam car I ever saw,'' he bellowed. ''Why'nt you ever buy new shocks?'' He fought against the motion and assembled his shotgun. Up ahead, the bike had to wait behind a yellow Subaru until an oncoming truck passed. We picked up fifty yards.

''Lift up your leg,'' Cowboy called. I did, and he pulled the Ruger free, checked the cylinder, then put it under his own thigh. He poked the shotgun barrel out the open window, rested the butt in his lap, and melted bonelessly into the worn seat. ''Okay, Rafferty,'' he called, ''you can catch him now.''

''If you're sure you're ready.''

We screamed along like that for five miles. I couldn't haul in the bike and he couldn't get away. I tried not to think about what the chase was doing to the Mustang's innards. Or to the right front tire I had been meaning to replace.

The bike wouldn't go any faster than the Mustang, but it sure could stop. When I realized he was slowing, I stood on the brakes. Even so, we almost hit him.

Then, cursing myself for stupidity, I accelerated and *tried* to hit him. Too late. He was on the loud pedal, too, turning smoothly into a side road. I wallowed through the corner with the tires yowling, off-line, and caught in the wrong gear.

''You ain't quite ready for Daytona yet, ace,'' Cowboy said.

I snarled an insult at him and flogged the Mustang after the biker.

The new road was paved, but once you'd said that, you'd covered all its good points. It was narrow—about a lane and a half—and twisty and hilly and the shoulders were in terrible shape. But for all the difficulty I had with that goat track, it seemed to be worse for the bike. We started to catch him.

"Won't be long now," Cowboy shouted.

"I want him alive."

"Yeah, I figured that. You'll just have to get me closer, that's all."

The rider looked back at us each time we came to a straight stretch. I thought he was the one who had nudged Turk and laughed at Fran and me, but I couldn't be sure with the slipstream blowing his long hair around his head.

A left-hand bend tightened up suddenly. I had to straighten the wheel and brake savagely for ten yards to make it around. Then I missed a shift coming out of the corner. After that, the gearbox growled more loudly than normal.

A mile farther along, where the road skirted a wooded hill, we picked up ground on the bike. Rapidly. Blue smoke came from the motorcycle's exhaust and, for the first time in miles, the rider sat bolt upright.

Cowboy crowed. "We got him! He blowed it up."

He hadn't, though. He slowed to a crawl, bounced the heavy bike in and out of the ditch, and faded into the tree-covered hillside at full throttle. I got a quick glimpse of his back wheel spewing dirt and grass clumps, then I was too busy getting the Mustang stopped to watch.

Cowboy leaped out, carrying the shotgun. He ran back to where the bike had disappeared. I started to back up, but the Mustang bucked and stalled. There was a evil hissing sound under the hood.

Cowboy fired twice with the shotgun. Shredded leaves drifted away in the wind and a wrist-sized branch twenty yards uphill jerked and hung askew.

"Shit!" Cowboy said. "I can't see for the scrub."

After a few moments, when the ear-ringing blasts had died away, we could hear the bike, growling and farting and screaming somewhere in the woods as it clawed its way up the hillside.

Cowboy slapped his leg with his hat and swore. "Look at that hill, Rafferty! How steep you reckon that is?"

"I don't know. Forty degrees? Fifty? Who the hell cares?"

"Well, goddamn it, did you see how he got away? Did you? It ain't fair!"

"Calm down, for Christ's sake." The hissing from the Mustang was louder now. I opened the hood and stepped back quickly when steam billowed out. Cowboy trudged over and leaned against the trunk. He was a picture of dejection.

"Cowboy," I said, "don't worry about it. If one biker is here, they're all here. We'll find them now."

"It ain't that. It's that goddamned motorcycle. Did you see it go up that hill?" He looked at me with mournful eyes. "Rafferty, there ain't no way in the world a horse could do that!"

CHAPTER TWENTY-ONE

It was after six o'clock before the Mustang had cooled enough to be driven. When we got underway, the transmission sounded terrible. Surprisingly, all the gears worked.

There was a motel in town, after all. Conover Court had twelve rooms butted together in a single wing that ran back from a brick office and manager's house. The house was neat and newish. The motel wing was timber. It needed paint.

The manager was an oafish glad-hander with thinning hair and metal-rimmed eyeglasses. He gave us Room Six, in the middle of the wing. It had twin beds, a small bathroom, a bedside table, and two uncomfortable-looking straight chairs. It was clean. It was also noisy.

"What the . . ." Cowboy said.

Television game show squeals and applause came through the plasterboard wall. The Davis family won something. They sounded fairly excited about it.

"Country motel version of cable TV," I said. "A set in every third room."

"Well, I ain't gonna listen to that crap all night," Cowboy said. "Gimme that key."

He returned with the key to Room Twelve and we moved to the end of the wing. It was the same inside, except quieter. Sometime in the last year or two, the local hardware store had discounted their paint stock. The salmon color had been a big seller.

Cowboy went out for beer and hamburgers. I phoned Hilda in Dallas.

"Hi, big guy," she said. "How goes the quest?"

"Not so bad. We found one of them." I told her about it and she seemed relieved at the anticlimax. "How are you?" I said.

"Okay. I took Fran to that Zifretti boy's funeral this afternoon. She cried."

"I don't know if that was such a good idea," I said. "See anybody strange there?"

"Only that cop you know. The one who dresses like Nathan Detroit."

"Ricco."

"Right," she said. "What's wrong?"

"Nothing, probably. We seem to have the bikers cornered in this end of north Texas, so I guess there's no harm done."

"Cornered?"

"Never mind, smart-ass. How's Fran now?"

"Oh, she's fine. She's a little worried about a job interview tomorrow, but she'll be okay. Remember Beth Richards? The woman who bought that Georgian bookcase? She may give Fran a job in her gift shop."

"Good. Thanks very much."

"Nothing to it," she said. "I think I like Fran, now that I've gotten to know her."

"Something wrong with this phone," I said. "Aren't you the broad who hates living with other women?"

"I said I liked her. I didn't say I want to take her to raise."

"Fair enough. Look, babe, I'm going to be stuck out here for another day or three. I'll call you tomorrow night, if I can."

"Okay. Be careful."

"There's another way?"

* * *

After we ate, and after Cowboy called Mimi to check on the new foal, we cruised through Conover. It didn't take very long.

There were three carloads of teenage boys making the rounds, too. They would start near the motel, drive the mile and a half into town, around the square, out the highway, U-turn, and repeat the circuit.

"Did you do that as a kid, Cowboy?"

He nodded. "We called it cruising Main."

"We called it dragging the gut, as I recall."

"Well, it ain't got anymore sensible since those days," Cowboy said. "Let's quit."

"Quit? Why, we might get to pick up Mary Lou Hoffstetter. I think she'll put out."

Cowboy grinned. "Yeah, guy told me she blew the whole football team after practice last week."

"Mary Lou did that? And all I've been asking her to do is my algebra homework."

"Aw, you goody-goodies never get laid. Everybody knows that."

"Not only that, I better quit playing with it, too. I think my eyes are going."

Who says you can't relive the good old days?

We tried the drive-in and drove to the beer joint Billy Dolan had mentioned, but didn't see any sign of bikers.

On the way back, third gear sounded like a blender chopping walnuts, so we gave up for the night.

"Outlaw bikers oughta stand out like a dog's balls in a piss-ant burg like this," Cowboy grumbled from the bathroom. "Opposition's out there somewhere. Why can't we catch 'em? It just don't feel right."

We slept with our shotguns on the floor beside our beds.

In the morning, Cowboy went cruising again, while I used the motel phone to work through the newspaper ad responses. There were two from the Conover area.

The first was a screechy housewife who wanted to know what right I had to bad-mouth motorcycles; didn't I know lots of honest folks enjoyed trail-bike riding; her Leroy was third runner-up in last year's Dalton County moto-cross and you wouldn't find a nicer boy anywhere, besides which he got good grades and didn't hang around beer joints or read dirty books. So there.

The other call had come from a woman named Arbetha Fullylove. She wanted to talk, too, but she wanted to do it her way.

When Cowboy returned, we checked out of the motel and drove to the Abyssinian Faith Tabernacle. It was a tiny caricature of a turn-of-the-century church, spotlessly white and toylike in the exact center of a small lot two blocks west of the town square.

"Look at that," Cowboy said, as he got out of the car. "There was a nigger church like this back home."

A tall, dignified black man in a white shirt met us at the door. He took us inside to meet Arbetha. There were rows of folding chairs instead of pews. We sat up front, near an old piano.

Arbetha Fullylove was a brown pixy with a round, seamed face. She was eighty, at least, and she wore an immaculate black dress with imitation pearl buttons down the front. A zipper had been sewn in and a loop of red ribbon threaded through the zipper tab. Her hands were thick-knuckled and heavily veined. She held them in her lap and they shook continually.

"Reverend Daniels thinks ah'm a silly old woman," she said. "But when ah seen your ad in the paper, ah figgered somebody got to do somethin' 'bout those men works for Greedy. Else folks do, why, they gonna hurt someone real bad one day."

Daniels patted her twitchy hands and said, "Now, Sister Arbetha, you be careful about such accusations." His voice was low and melodic.

"Be careful, hah!" she said. "Mebbe you think ah knocked mah-self down mah own front steps?"

The reverend pursed his lips and didn't say anything.

"What's the matter you, Reverend? Whose side you on?" the old woman said.

I looked at Daniels. He leaned back in his chair and frowned. I guess we were both trying to figure out whose side he was on.

"Tell me about it," I said to Arbetha Fullylove.

"Greedy sent them motor-sickle men to scare me off," she said indignantly. "Imagine! Forty-two years in that house, since way back afore Albert died, and he thinks ah'd sell out now."

"Who is Greedy?" I asked.

Arbetha cackled. "Greedy's greedy, thass who's greedy. That man got the sickness of greed runnin' right through his hell-bound body, yes, sir!"

Reverend Daniels said, "T. J. MacCready is a local businessman."

"White trash, thass all he is, Reverend, and you knows it!"

Cowboy said, "MacCready's got an office down from the post office. Noticed it this morning. His sign says Investments and Property."

Daniels nodded. "That's correct. Mr. MacCready owns a lot of property around Conover."

"Okay," I said. "Now, Mrs. Fullylove, you said MacCready wants to buy your house?"

"He shore do! Offered me twenny-four thousand dollars cash money fer it, too. That's a powerful lot, but ah cain't leave mah home!"

"Why?"

"Cos ah live there!"

"No, I didn't mean that. Why would MacCready want your house badly enough to use strong-arm tactics?"

"The good Lord only knows," she said. "Ah don't."

"Mr. MacCready owns all the other houses and lots on Austin Street," Daniels said. "Certainly, he wants to buy Sister Arbetha's property, but . . ." He shrugged expressively.

Cowboy said, "Tell us about the men who pestered you, gal."

"Don't you *gal* me, young man! I'se old enough to be your grandma."

"I surely do apologize, ma'am," Cowboy said.

Arbetha nodded shortly and shifted in her seat to turn away from Cowboy. "They was motor-sickle men." She waved her shaky hands at eye level. "A great big one, bald as that po-liceman on the TV. And mean lookin'. T'other one was fat and dirty. Hair all over his face. They come around on a Sat'day 'bout two months ago. Jest walked in, struttin' and talkin' dirty, you know. They say things like, 'Whyn't you get outa this old dump?' and 'Niggers oughta go back where they come from.' Stuff like that. That fat one, he pushed over a table in mah sittin' room. And he done his business in the corner, like an old tom cat."

"Did they mention this MacCready by name?"

She thought about it. "No," she said finally. "I'se got to be fair 'bout that. They didn't say nothin' about Greedy, but thass who they was workin' for. Ah could tell."

"All right. And they knocked you down?"

"They shore did. The fat one, he gone back outside, see. Ah was out on mah porch, tellin' him don't never come back, when the tall one, he just walk out past me like ah was nothin'. Pushin' past me, like. Ah fall down the steps, hurt mah knee. The fat one laugh. Then they get on their motor-sickles and they go off makin' that squeally sound like they do."

I thanked her and we shook hands. It was like holding a warm, angry crab.

"You catch them motor-sickle men, you boys thump 'em for me, promise?"

"Yes, ma'am," Cowboy said. "We surely will."

Daniels walked us out. We stood on the sparse lawn. Cowboy put on his hat and tilted it forward over his eyes. "Greedy MacCready," he said. "I suppose everybody calls him that?"

Daniels nodded deliberately. "Not to his face, you understand."

"No, I reckon not," Cowboy said. "Man like that, in a town like this, he's got friends, I'd say. The local banker, for sure. Probably most of the city council, too. And the local police."

"No police here," Daniels said. "Conover's not incorporated. All we have is a town constable. He rents his house from MacCready."

I said, "So Mrs. Fullylove didn't report the incident to the constable."

Daniels and Cowboy gave me identical looks.

"County sheriff?"

"Sister Arbetha would make a poor witness against MacCready," Daniels said flatly. "Even if what she says is true, folks know she's fallen off that porch before. When she was alone." He looked me in the eye and said, "White folks here don't mess with MacCready. I don't want Sister Arbetha to do it, either."

"Forget her for a minute," I said. "Does the sound of MacCready hiring bikers as muscle ring true?"

Daniels looked away. "Folks have had problems before," he said. "Bank trouble, sometimes. And cut fences and fires, things like that. Old Mister Prescott didn't want to sell. He had problems right up to the day they found his body under his tractor. MacCready has a tenant farmer on that land now, and he doesn't seem to have any problems at all."

"Was Prescott black or white?"

Daniels laughed sourly. "He was white, but that doesn't matter. Conover's integrated. Black or white, if folks don't want what MacCready wants, they tend to be unlucky."

"Yeah," I said. "I can see how that would be the case."

Cowboy said, "Yeah," too, and we shook hands with Reverend Daniels and we got into the car and drove off.

Cowboy looked out at sleepy little Conover. There was a lot of hate in that look.

"It's a mite early for lunch," he said. "How 'bout we go whup the living hell out of MacCready to work up an appetite?"

CHAPTER TWENTY-TWO

Crooks are just like cops: you can never find one when you need him.

MacCready's office was a small, cream-colored wooden building. It was set on oddly high foundations, so the front door was three steps up from the street. There was a brick building with a lawyer's sign close by on one side of MacCready's; a vacant lot, then an old house on the other.

MacCready's door was locked. I knocked. No answer. We pressed our noses against the glass panes. Inside, there was an old wooden desk, an older wooden office chair, a worn leather couch, and four starkly modern steel file cabinets set against a wall. There was another room in the back. Most of that room was out of sight.

Except for the file cabinets, MacCready's office looked down-home, old-fashioned, broken-in, and comfortable. I liked it a lot better than my own office. Personally, I wouldn't keep pictures of myself shaking hands with state bigwigs on the wall, but some people like that sort of thing.

Cowboy wandered around the side of MacCready's building. I sat on the front steps. A pickup truck with brown feed sacks in the back blatted past. The driver worked hard at ignoring me.

Cowboy returned. "Back door's locked, too," he said.

"Looks like he's got a storeroom and toilet back there. Little alley runs through there. Two parking spaces. No car now, though."

"We can't break in," I said. "Somebody would spot us in a minute out here."

"Back's no good, either. There's a nosy old broad hanging laundry across the alley. She got real interested when I tried the door."

"Come on, let's find a phone book."

MacCready, T. J., was listed, but the address was simply Route 1, Conover. I started into the drugstore, expecting to find out where MacCready lived in two minutes. Cowboy didn't like the idea.

"Town's too small," he said. "Hell, they already made us, I reckon. Everybody knows there are two strangers in town. By now, the smart ones know we're huntin'. You let on we want to find MacCready, why, they'll warn him before you get out of sight." He shook his head. "I know these little towns. If you want MacCready to run, you go ask where he is."

"Oh," I said. "That was probably Lesson Eight in the Private-Investigation-Made-Easy course. The post office lost that one."

"No need to get upset," he said. "I'm just telling you about small towns, that's all."

"Thank you, Thorton Wilder."

"Aw, the hell with it. C'mon, boss, it's time to feed me. 'Fore I complain to the shop steward."

We ate breaded cardboard disguised as veal cutlets, gray cole slaw, and runny mashed potatoes. The sign said Home Style Cooking. Apparently it meant the kind of home with bars on the windows.

The afternoon drifted away in a haze of heat and boredom. Twice, people walked up MacCready's steps and tried his door. MacCready didn't show.

By 4:30, a freckled ten-year-old had spent an hour watching us watch MacCready's office. "Let's go," I said. "You're right. This goddamned town's too small for a stakeout."

Smiley, the motel manager, gave us Room Twelve for another night. We showered away the sweat and dust, and hit the street again.

Cowboy drove for a change. We cruised up and down country roads, read mailboxes, wished for bikers. No bikers. No MacCready. Nothing.

At dusk, we filled the Mustang with gas again, surrounded another forgettable meal, and went back to the motel.

"Want to hit MacCready's office tonight?" Cowboy asked.

"Naw, but tomorrow we have to make a move. This is taking too long. If MacCready doesn't show in the morning, we'll ask around, even if it does spook him. There must be at least one person in the local establishment who hates MacCready's guts."

Cowboy checked his shotgun, laid it beside his bed, and propped himself against the pillow. "Whatever you say, boss-man." He opened a copy of *Western Horseman*.

I tried Hilda's number. No answer.

Tomorrow, I thought. Tomorrow we'll blow this stupid town wide open if we have to.

I needn't have worried about it.

That night, the bikers came to us.

CHAPTER TWENTY-THREE

They didn't make much noise, but it was enough to bring me out of a deep sleep in the middle of the night. The first sound I recognized was a boot scrape on gravel.

"Cowboy," I whispered.

"I hear 'em," he said. There was a sharp click from his side of the room.

I slowly eased my shotgun off the floor and pointed it past my toes, toward the only door to the room. The moon was up and a little light filtered through the curtains. Not much; only a gray wash that softened and changed objects without hiding them.

When I was a young boy, it used to scare the living hell out of me to wake up in that menacing gloom.

There was a hoarse whisper outside, too soft to understand. Then someone kicked the door, hard, beside the lock. It splintered, gave way on the second kick, and flew open against the wall.

One of the fat, hairy ones charged through the open doorway, howling as he came. I shot him in the chest.

The biker stopped short. He swayed backward, still clutching a rifle or shotgun, and seemed about to catch his balance. Cowboy's shotgun went off and the biker collapsed with the right side of his head missing.

I rolled onto the floor between the beds; Cowboy arrived at the same time.

There were surprised shouts in the parking lot. A square shape flew in through the gaping doorway, bounced off the dead biker with a muffled sound, and fell onto the thin carpet. Dimly, behind the ringing in my ears, I heard a rhythmic sloshing.

Then I smelled the gas fumes.

"Hey, now," Cowboy said, "these old boys are serious." He went up and over his bed in a fluid roll. I heard him scuttle into the bathroom. Glass broke and rattled on the tile floor. There were eight or ten sharp flat cracks, rapid and evenly spaced, then Cowboy's shotgun boomed twice.

"Back's covered," he called from the other side of the bed a minute later. "Automatic weapon."

The gas fumes were stronger now. "There'll be a torch coming in here soon," I said.

"No shit," Cowboy said laconically. "Throw my stuff over here. Boots first. Let's see how thin that wall really is."

I tossed his boots over the bed, heard him grunt when one struck him. His bag was open and I removed his Ruger before I threw it after the boots. A burst of automatic fire exploded the window beside the open door and *spat-spatted* into the wall above the beds.

When the firing stopped, I followed Cowboy's boots and bag over the bed. My hands were full of guns and my bare butt felt cold and exposed.

"Keep 'em honest," Cowboy said, about the same time I thought of it, and I put a round of buckshot through the doorway. Someone screamed an indecipherable taunt.

Cowboy, flat on his back in underwear and boots, held his shotgun as far from the wall as he could and fired twice. Two saucer-sized holes appeared in the wall six inches above the floor. Cowboy scootched forward and kicked at the edges of the holes.

A burly figure darted past the doorway. I snapped a shot

at it, missed, and fumbled for shells. "Here," Cowboy grunted, "do mine, too."

I topped up both shotguns, stuffed Cowboy's Ruger into his bag, and made sure the .45 was in my bag.

There was a shifting orange glow outside. "Hurry it up, Cowboy," I said.

"Almost ready." He stopped kicking, reversed himself, and jammed his head and shoulders into the hole. He stuck, wriggled convulsively, and disappeared into the next room.

I threw things after him. His bag and my bag; for the guns, not the clothes. Then the shotguns and finally—as a fireball arced into the room—me.

The ragged hole in the plasterboard had sturdy two-by-fours on each side. I think sixteen inches is the standard distance between studs in a wall. At a guess, I would have said I could not fit through a hole sixteen inches wide.

I was wrong. I went through there like a rat up a drainpipe. While I did, I heard a dull *crump* and felt sudden heat like a bad sunburn on my legs.

The room we entered had not been rented for the night. I stood there, naked, trembling a little from exertion and adrenaline. Cowboy came back from the window. He had to shout to be heard over the blast furnace in our room. "Keep moving," he said. "I reckon this whole place is gonna go."

We went through more walls, learning on the way. We found the small table near the beds was exactly the right size to fit between the studs. If you swung the table hard enough, the plasterboard would break up into dusty plate-sized chunks. It took about six good whacks per wall. After two walls, the table legs came off in your hands.

The second room we broke into had been occupied until the commotion frightened everyone but us outside. We stopped there to get dressed in the clothes we had left. What we didn't have, we stole. I found a shirt and put it on. Cowboy liberated a pair of socks.

The third room was empty. In the fourth, I took a pair of Puma joggers only one size too big.

When we crawled into the fifth room, there was a roar of motorcycles outside. We got to the door in time to see two bike brake lights wink as they paused, then turned onto the highway.

"Party's over, I guess," said Cowboy.

We brushed plaster dust off each other and stepped outside with "who, me?" looks on our faces. As we did, an elderly fire truck wheezed into the motel parking lot. Cowboy and I strolled toward the Mustang.

The Room Twelve end of the motel had crumpled into a bed of fierce coals. The rest of the wing was progressively collapsing as the fire worked its way through the flimsy wooden building.

There was a small crowd of ten or fifteen people gawking at the fire. Cowboy and I eased around behind them. It wasn't easy to be invisible while lugging shotguns and pistols and wearing other people's clothes, but we gave it a good shot.

The Mustang was on the far side of the small parking lot; close enough to the fire to be uncomfortably hot. I retrieved my spare key from the magnetic box under the fender and she reluctantly started.

"That's gonna cost you," Cowboy said, as I wheeled the car out of our parking spot and bumped over a fire hose. "Nail ripped the hell out of my boot."

"Put a new pair on the bill," I said. "Mollison can afford it."

"Pure elk hide, too," he grumped. "And just broke in good. Damn!"

A chocolate-brown LTD was parked beside the highway, opposite the motel entrance. The driver was alone in the car. He sat watching the fire. He glanced at us, looked away, then jerked his head back in a silent movie double-take.

The LTD started with a roar and spat gravel as it lurched onto the road. The lights came on and I saw the personalized license plate: MAC 1.

The LTD was probably thirty miles an hour faster than my tired old Mustang. That didn't do it any good at all.

MacCready drove it off the road half a mile later.

CHAPTER TWENTY-FOUR

MacCready's driving was pathetic. He lost it on a straight stretch of road, for God's sake. He leaned the LTD up against a telephone pole with the left rear wheel hanging in space above the drainage ditch, then he raced the motor and tried to drive away.

"Simple shit, ain't he?" Cowboy said.

MacCready saw me walk toward his car and he slapped the door lock button down like a tourist in South Dallas after midnight.

I pointed the shotgun at him and motioned him out of the car. He looked stubborn and didn't move, so I blew out the back window. He came out of the car in a scrambling rush, fell into the ditch, and clambered onto the road with his hands held high and his pant legs dark and dripping.

"What the—" he said. "You can't get away with—"

"Oh, shut up, MacCready. Get in the Mustang."

"MacCready? Who's MacCready? I'm not—"

"Will you give it a rest, for Christ's sake?" I said. "Which would you rather be: MacCready or dead?"

"Okay, okay. Take it easy, boys. We can work this out."

Cowboy drove, MacCready sat in the front passenger seat with his hands flat on the dashboard, and I sat in the back.

"I don't know what you boys want with me," MacCready said. His voice quavered a little.

I said, "All you need to know is that if you move your hands off the dashboard, I will hurt you very badly. Do you believe that?"

He nodded slowly.

"Okay." I said. "Cowboy, find someplace where we can talk to Greedy without being disturbed."

Cowboy drove through Conover and continued east on Texas 11. He took the side road where the biker had eluded us and tried a gravel road to the north. It was a driveway. He tried again. The second gravel road led us a mile or two into the woods.

The road stopped at a circular lake three hundred yards across. There was a ten-foot-square corrugated metal building at the water's edge. A pipe came out of the lake, ran through the building, and dove underground.

Cowboy turned off the ignition. The Mustang pinged and tinkled in the stillness. There was a full moon. There were no other buildings or lights in sight.

"Out," I said. MacCready and Cowboy got out. I followed.

MacCready stood quietly by the car. He brushed his hands, straightened his suit, shook his soggy feet. He was a short, sleek man in his late forties with a vulpine face and dark hair that looked oily in the flat moonlight. He wore glasses with thin metal rims.

He had calmed down during the ride. When I waved him away from the car, he came with his hands outspread and a good-ole-boy wheeler-dealer tone in his voice. "Look here, I don't know what the problem is, but we can sure—"

I ignored him and spoke to Cowboy. "The thing that pisses me off," I said, "is that now we have to drag the information about these bikers out of him. I hope we get paid for the extra work, after all this."

"Heyyy," MacCready said.

"Can't be helped," Cowboy said. "You know what the Old Man said."

"Yeah, but I don't have to like it."

MacCready said "Heyyy" again.

"You see, MacCready," I said, "it's supposed to look like a thrill killing, right? Like a psycho did it. This kind of contract is always messy, but we don't mind that. Then this biker business came up. The Man wants to know who they are, so . . . And wouldn't you know it, before we could run that down, you sent those freaks after us at the motel. So we have a personal stake in it now."

MacCready tried to run. He lurched clumsily around the front of the Mustang and lumbered toward the surrounding forest. Cowboy loped after him, kicked him on the side of the knee, and MacCready crumpled to the ground.

I walked over and knelt beside him. "Here's the very best I can offer you," I said. "Tell us about the bikers. Before we cut you, I'll give you a little tap to put you to sleep."

"You're crazy," MacCready wheezed, holding his knee.

Cowboy laughed. It was a helluva good laugh. It even made me shiver. MacCready took it to heart. There was a sudden sharp urine smell in the air.

"They weren't supposed to go that far," he said in a flat, resigned tone. "I heard about two strangers in a beat-up old Mustang watching my office. They said you had bothered them in Dallas, too. But, I swear, they were only supposed to scare you off. All that shooting . . . and the fire . . . I didn't know that was going to happen."

"Start at the beginning, Greedy. Who is the bald one? The one they call Turk."

"Dixon," MacCready said. "Ivan Dixon. He's crazy, too." Presumably he meant "too" as in like me.

"He runs the gang, does he?"

MacCready nodded vigorously. "Yes. He's one of the Dixon boys. From up around Mount Pleasant."

"How did you get connected with them?"

"I bought the Dixon place after Ivan's uncle died. Ivan— Turk—inherited it. I bought it from him. He came up here early last year, from someplace down south. Houston or Galveston, I don't know. He had other gang riders with him. I guess they're still living on the money from the farm, mostly.''

"Mostly? You use them for odd jobs, don't you?"

"Nothing like tonight, I swear. I didn't know what they were going to do. Honest.''

"Sure," I said. "There were five I know of, Greedy. Couple are dead already. And we killed one tonight. Which two rode away from the motel?''

"Turk," he said, "and Joe Lockhart. They call him Smokey Joe.''

So it was Stomper who had charged into our shotguns.

"Okay. You're doing fine." I reached out to pat him on the shoulder. He jerked back and crawled a few feet away.

Cowboy stood over MacCready. "Where did they go?" he asked.

"I don't know. Honest."

"Guess," I said. "Remember, there's a nice prize for being right.''

"They stay at a place south of town," he said. "The old Prescott place.''

"I heard you had a tenant farmer there."

"Yes," he said, "but Wiley only farms it. He lives at his own place down the road. Turk Dixon and his friends use the Prescott house. They keep an eye on the place for me.''

"You're bullshitting us," I said. "If those animals had been living out there for better than a year, the whole county would know it.''

"No," MacCready whined. "It's true! We have a deal. They take it easy around town. Low profile, that's what I told them.''

"He's lying," I said to Cowboy. "Let's get started."

MacCready screamed like a hurt woman. "I swear!" he wailed. "They're gone most of the time, but that's where they live. Please!''

It was starting to get light by then. The little lake had taken on a pewter shade. Trees on the far side were sharp against the eastern sky.

Cowboy jerked his head at me and we walked away from MacCready to talk.

"I know we're only funning him about a hit," he said, "but you ought to consider it."

"Hell, Cowboy, what's the point? Without the bikers, he's not a threat."

"Point is, if he gets to Turk and Smokey Joe before we do, we'll never catch those old boys."

"I don't think Greedy will be interested in talking to them. He'll be too busy remembering how he wet himself hoping he wouldn't be awake when his throat got cut."

"Another thing," Cowboy said. "I know these Greedy MacCready characters. We can scare him off for a while. Won't be long, though, he'll be back in business, leaning on honest folks."

"Maybe. I can't help that. I'm not going to kill him just because he's the local General Bullmoose."

"You're a pushover sometimes, Rafferty."

"It's my genuine love for all mankind."

"You gotta do something about that," Cowboy said.

He walked to the car and slid into the passenger seat. I got in, too. After the Mustang groaned into life, I turned it around and started up the gravel road. MacCready struggled to his feet and limped down to the water's edge.

The last thing I saw in the rearview mirror was Mac-Cready, bending over with his hands on his knees, throwing up on his shoes.

CHAPTER TWENTY-FIVE

On the way back through Conover, we stopped at the drive-in cafe opposite Dolan Ford. We only intended to ask directions to the Prescott farm, but a booth by the window looked comfortable and the coffee smelled good and it seemed a shame the cook had nothing to do. So we ordered breakfast.

A breezy waitress brought black coffee first. It tasted great, but it felt odd to drink morning coffee without smoking. I'd salvaged my wallet from the motel fire, but lost my pipe and tobacco pouch. Lousy priorities.

"If you smoked," I said to Cowboy, "I could bum a cigarette."

"Filthy habit." He shrugged. "Buy a pack if you're hurting."

"Naw. I'll tough it out."

By the time our food came, the place had started to fill up. Leathery men hunched over coffee cups and dutifully wise-cracked with the waitress. Outside, a sunburned man in creased jeans stepped out of his pickup. He gave the Mustang an odd look as he ambled past. When he came in, he looked at us, too, then sat at the counter with another local. They had their heads together most of the time.

"We got to get out of this town," Cowboy said. "Every

goddamn person in the county knows us one way or another.''

"Blend in," I said. "Chew a stalk of grass. Stub your toe in the dust. Practice saying "aw, shucks" and "reckon it might rain?''

Cowboy shook his head. "City boys," he said disdainfully. "You're bigger hicks than us country people."

"Guilty," I said.

We finished our food and I sent the waitress away when she offered more coffee. I wanted a smoke too badly and I didn't want to give in and buy cigarettes.

"Come on," I said to Cowboy, "let's get it done."

The Prescott place was an undersized, single-story, once-white frame house set in a U-shaped windbreak of elm trees. The home site was surrounded by fields that looked pretty good to me, not that I knew what I was looking at. Inside the windbreak, though, the house and grounds had a beaten, weary look.

We drove by the first time without stopping. The only sign of activity was a quarter-mile away, where a green tractor crawled along a fence line doing something agricultural.

On the second pass, I stopped on the road, out of sight from the house. Cowboy got out, went through a barbed wire fence, and ran across a plowed field, angling toward the rear of the house. He had the Ruger tucked into the back of his belt. He carried his shotgun in high port position across his chest.

I turned past the mailbox as fast as I could and urged the Mustang to do its feeble imitation of acceleration up the drive. There were no shots from the house, which was a welcome surprise.

I drove as close to the house as I could, bailed out carrying my Ithaca, and flattened against the front wall. Still no response.

I peeked around the corner. Cowboy came from behind a shed and darted out of view around the back of the house.

I began to have a small empty feeling in the pit of my stomach.

We hit the front and back doors together and found ourselves facing each other down a hallway that ran the length of the house. At Cowboy's end, the hall opened into a room, probably the kitchen. There were two doors on the right side of the hall, one door on the left.

The hallway walls were covered with motorcycle posters and graffiti. The floor was littered with cigarette butts and empty beer cans. And dirt. It might have been swept once in the past year, but certainly not twice.

I went through the doorway on the left with the shotgun ready. Living room. Another door connected it to the kitchen. Cowboy poked his head through, then disappeared.

The living room was empty, except for two threadbare couches and a nearly new color television set. There was a nice collection of cans and butts on the floor there, too.

When I came out of the living room, one of the other hallway doors opened. I nearly sprained my back bringing the shotgun to bear.

"Oh!" she said. "Shit, you scared me!"

She was a pudgy girl of about eighteen, with tangled brown hair and a heavy jaw. She wore a T-shirt with a screen print of a starving baby and the words Ethiopian Slimming Salon on it. The T-shirt stopped just below her crotch. Her naked thighs were heavy and lard-white.

Cowboy appeared, jerked her out of the doorway and dove into the room. I went down the hall and kicked open the last door. It was an empty bedroom.

"Empty," Cowboy called.

"Here, too," I said.

"What the fuck do you guys want?" asked Thunder Thighs.

"Turk and Smokey," I said. "Where are they?"

"Fuck should I know?" She yawned into a grubby fist. "What time is it?"

"Early," I said. "When did they leave?"

She shrugged with an exaggerated gesture that showed

she didn't wear panties and didn't care who knew it. "One, two o'clock. So what? You pigs got a warrant?"

"We don't need a warrant," I said. "We're not cops."

"Oh," said Thunder Thighs, "that's different." She walked into the living room, switched on the TV set, and sprawled on a couch. When the TV screen settled, the Roadrunner did it to the Coyote again.

I felt like the Coyote.

"Come on," said Cowboy. We went to the kitchen. I closed the door to the living room. Cowboy gently laid his shotgun on a linoleum-covered counter and glared out a window into the empty backyard. "We fucked up," he said.

"A reasonable summation."

"Probably shouldn't have had breakfast."

"I don't think it mattered," I said. "They haven't been back here since they left for the motel."

Cowboy snorted. "Does that bitch strike you as reliable, boss-man?"

"Look at it this way. Does she look as if she gives a shit either way?"

Cowboy pointed his finger at me. "You got a good point there."

Thunder Thighs shoved open the door, shuffled into the kitchen, and rummaged through the noisy old refrigerator. She muttered to herself, found a cold frankfurter, and bit the end off it.

"Gotta have my breakfast," she said. "Not worth squat without it. Hey, if the guys come back, there's gonna be shooting and all that, eh?"

"Most likely," said Cowboy.

"Well, what I mean is, you guys will give me a chance to get out of the way, won'tcha?"

"Yeah," I said. "Don't worry about it."

"Okay, thanks. See ya." She went out again. Her legs didn't look any better from the back.

"Come here," Cowboy said. "Want to show you something in that bedroom."

The room he had checked was similar to the one I had

seen; there were old mattresses and sleeping bags on the
floor, piles of clothing, and more motorcycle pinups.

The only difference was cultural and artistic; the room
he cleared had a Polaroid pornography display.

The photos were stuck to the wall with a mixture of
thumbtacks and tape. Some were obviously older than others. The settings varied, as did the participants, although
the theme was consistent. Each photo showed a biker having sex with one or more girls.

The bikers invariably mugged for the camera. The girls'
reactions were more varied. There was a chesty brunette
who specialized in poorly faked passion. Thunder Thighs
displayed only token politeness. A young girl with scarred
cheeks and a punk hairstyle appeared to be sleeping.

There were other photos, with other girls and other
expressions. The saddest of them all were the pictures of
Vivian Mollison.

"What we have here, Watson," I said, "is your basic,
grade A, legal evidence."

"Thought you might like 'em," Cowboy said. "This
one down here is your client, I guess."

"Yeah. Poor kid."

"She don't look very interested, does she?"

Vivian didn't look interested at all. She had the same
look in all seven photos; a vacuous docility that made her
look stupid. She seemed remote from what she was doing.
She might have been holding a banana or eating a popsicle
or simply daydreaming.

They were the most off-putting pictures of naked people
I had ever seen.

"How 'bout that ex-biker chickie in Dallas? I don't see
her in here," Cowboy said.

"Damned well better not," I said. I felt slightly ashamed
because I, too, had looked for photos of Fran.

Cartoon music came from the television set in the other
room while Cowboy and I took down the pictures of Vivian. I put them in my pocket.

"So, what do we do now, boss?"

"Rule Three," I said. "When all else fails, sit on your duff and await good news."

"One of your better rules," said Cowboy. "And for two-fifty a day, I'm a good sitter."

So, we sat on our duffs and waited for Turk and Smokey Joe to come home.

CHAPTER TWENTY-SIX

I moved the Mustang behind the house where it could not be seen from the road. Then we mapped out killing zones and paced off distances to the places we thought the bikers might stop when they arrived. We knocked a hole in a bedroom wall for a gunport.

On the television front, Thunder Thighs didn't give up when the morning cartoons ended; she dove straight into the soap operas.

Cowboy discovered a telephone under a pile of old magazines on the living room floor. I phoned the Dallas cop shop. Ed Durkee was in his office.

"I was beginning to wonder about you," he said. "Bring in the Rosencrantz broad. I'm catching a lot of flak over that Dew Drop Inn shooting."

"Okay, Ed, will do. Soon as I get back in town."

"Where the hell are you?"

"Dalton County," I said. "And the good part is, I have what you need for an arrest on the Mollison snatch."

"If you drag in some shit-kicker who claims he saw a motorcycle with a blonde on the back—"

"Better. The guys you want are Ivan Dixon—one of the Mount Pleasant Dixons, I'm told—and Joe, probably Joseph, Lockhart. Fran Rosencrantz can ID Dixon as the leader of the five bikers who bought Vivian Mollison from

Guts Holman. *And* I have snapshots of Dixon, Lockhart, and others in the sack with Vivian. How 'bout them apples?''

Ed grunted. I could imagine him rubbing his malleable face. "These pictures," he said. "Are we talking normal sex or rape?''

"Trust me. You've seen her since they let her go. Well, she looks even more spaced out in these photos. It might not be 'choke her down and black her eye' rape, but it's close enough for me. For the grand jury, too, I bet. Don't worry, Ed, you have a case.''

"Well, maybe . . .''

"Maybe, my ass! You'll have an eyewit to testify Dixon and his gang arrived without Vivian and left with her. You'll have photos of what they did with her. Plus medical and psychiatric reports about her condition afterward. What more do you want?''

"Well," he said, "having the bikers wouldn't hurt.''

"I'm working on that now." I told him where I was and that I expected Turk and Smokey Joe to return eventually. "With any luck, I'll deliver them this afternoon. You lucky devil. What would you do without me?''

"Goddamn it, Rafferty. You can't—does the county law out there know what you're doing?''

"Not exactly.''

"Listen, Rafferty, I did not answer this phone. You got that? Just bring in the Rosencrantz broad and don't tell me things I shouldn't know. Good-bye.''

"Hey! Did you get those names?''

"I got them. Dixon and Lockhart. I'll handle it. Go away.''

"Dixon's from Mount Pleasant. Try the—''

"Good-bye!" The phone went dead.

The thought of all that paperwork must have made him irritable.

I relieved Cowboy at the front window watch post. He dozed on one of the couches. Thunder Thighs was still encamped on the other couch, outstaring the television set. Her entertainment was briefly threatened when a newscast appeared instead of a soap. She found a game show on another channel. It was a close call.

Nothing happened outside. After two hours, I had enjoyed all the bucolic scenery I could stand and I badly needed a smoke. I shook Cowboy awake. He yawned and raised his eyebrows.

"Nada," I said. "I'll see if there's anything to eat in this dump."

There was nothing in the refrigerator that looked fresh enough to be consumed without a fight. In a cupboard over the sink, I found two cans of chili and one of beans. So far, so good.

Thunder Thighs trundled into the kitchen. "Oh, great," she said. "You fixing lunch?"

"If you can find a pan or two. And plates or bowls."

She opened drawers and looked under things and finally came up with an aluminum saucepan. It was encrusted with what may have been ancient spaghetti.

"Will this do?" she asked.

"It'll have to. Scrape out as much of that crap as you can."

She used a rusty table knife like a dagger and chipped hard pasta into the sink. I peeled the labels off the cans and set them aside. When the pan was down to merely filthy, I put the cans in and covered them with water from the hot water faucet. She showed me which stove burner worked and we waited for the water to boil.

"Don't you have to punch holes in the cans?" she asked. "Somebody told me you should do that, cause they'll explode otherwise."

"They would if you put them in a fire, but not this way. Think about it. Boiling water can't get hotter than 212 degrees, right?"

"I don't know."

"Take my word for it," I said. "They won't explode."

"Hey, that's really good then, isn't it? You wouldn't ever have to wash the pan, would you?"

Ain't science grand?

"Tell me something," I said. "Where did Turk get the automatic weapons?"

"Whatta you mean, army guns?"

"Yeah," I said. "Army guns."

"He bought them from a guy he knows. I think the guy stole them from a National Guard . . . What's that place where the army keeps guns? An arm . . ."

"A National Guard armory?"

"Yeah, that's it. And Turk got bullets and things, too."

"Any still around here?"

She went to look. While she was gone, the water boiled. As it did, it turned muddy brown from the debris in the pot. It was an effort to stay hungry.

When Thunder Thighs returned, she put a box of .223 ammo and an empty M16 magazine on the kitchen table. "Is this the stuff?" she said.

"That's it. Wait here." I took the ammunition and the magazine into the living room and showed them to Cowboy.

"Whoo-ee," he said. "And here I used to think bikers fought with ball bats and chains."

"Me, too, but those weren't hornets buzzing around last night."

"Wish I'd known this before," he said. "I'd have charged you more."

"Too late now. You want chili or beans for lunch?"

"Chili, I guess, long as what's-her-pussy don't cook it."

"Stand by for the blue-plate special."

There weren't any plates, blue or otherwise, but I found three spoons not quite ready for condemnation. I held them under the hot water faucet for a long time. Then I burned my fingers sawing the cans open with a beer opener.

Thunder Thighs wanted chili, but she settled for beans and gingerly carried the hot can to her nest in front of the TV.

I found a six-pack of Lone Star in the refrigerator and lugged the beer and chili into the living room. Cowboy and I leaned against the window frame, eating chili from the can with bent spoons. A TV quiz show yammered away in the background.

Ever wonder why the next generation isn't flocking into the private investigation business?

After lunch, I dozed awhile, relieved Cowboy at 1:00, and wondered when—and if—Turk and Smokey Joe would come back. I made it through my watch without a smoke, but I wasn't smiling much when Cowboy came on again at 3:00.

I was tired, bored, grubby, and beginning to think we had been skunked. And I was irritated at myself for wanting my nicotine so badly.

For something to do, I phoned my office and talked to the girl on duty at the answering service. Marge Mollison had called four times. She wanted me to get back to her as soon as possible.

Marge answered her phone on the second ring. She was wound up tight. Her voice had a bright, frantic edge to it.

"Where have you *been*?" she said. "We've waited for *hours*!"

"I'm out of town. Good news, though. We—"

"Uh oh," Cowboy said. "Trouble coming."

"Got to go, Marge. I'll call you back." I heard her howl as I dropped the phone on the cradle.

"Well, how about that," I said to Cowboy. "The bad guys finally got here, did they?"

"Worse," he said. "It's the *good* guys."

CHAPTER TWENTY-SEVEN

There were three blue Dalton County sheriff's cars in the front yard and two more on the road. A tall red-faced man in a tan Stetson stood behind one of the cars and yelled into a bullhorn. He had his mouth too close to the microphone, so the words came out muffled, but basically it was the same come-out-with-your-hands-up speech you hear every night on the late movie.

"Hope your client knows a bail bondsman," Cowboy grumbled.

"Look on the bright side," I said. "At least they don't have M16s."

"Got everything else, though. You ever see so many cops with riot guns? Three of 'em just ran around back. And look at that jerk over there, behind the tree. Man, don't he look like he wants to be a hero?"

Thunder Thighs looked over our shoulders, ran into the back bedroom, and slammed the door. Cowboy and I dropped our guns out the living room window, laced our fingers on top of our heads, and walked outside.

They let us look down riot gun barrels while they frisked us. Then they cuffed our hands behind our backs and tucked us into the rear seats of separate cruisers.

Three deputies stormed the house. They came out with Thunder Thighs. She held her hands over her head, which made the T-shirt ride high on her hips. A toothy deputy whistled and called to a friend of his. "Hey, Jack! She taking yer picture, hoss!"

The red-faced man bellowed at Thunder Thighs. "Lucille Billings, if your pappy could see you . . . *Put those arms down!* Hawkins, get her back inside. She must have somethin' else to wear. Then bring her in!"

I stuck my head out the window and asked Toothy, "That the sheriff?"

"A. K. Edson, finest sherf in North Texas," he said proudly.

Sheriff Edson was six-six, at least, and no more than two inches of that came from the high heels on his tooled leather boots. He wore tan twill, like his deputies, and a black leather gunbelt with a heavy revolver on the right side. His Stetson was centered an inch above white eyebrows, and he had a straight nose and a firm jaw. Edson was made for his job. He *looked* like a sheriff.

Remember, though, in Texas people elect their county sheriffs. Dressing up can be helpful imagewise, as they say around the courthouse.

Edson scowled at me and then at Cowboy. It was a pure John Wayne gotcha look. He folded himself into the passenger seat of an empty cruiser and waited impassively. A gray-haired deputy jumped behind the wheel.

It was time to go; Sheriff Edson's cruiser first, then mine, then Cowboy's, and finally my Mustang, driven by a pimply deputy who was perhaps only five years older than the car.

Toothy rode in the back seat beside me. The driver was a redhead with long sideburns.

"If you guys want to stop for a beer," I said, "I'll buy the first round."

"Shut up," said Toothy in a neutral voice.

"Funny thing," I said. "A fellow can really get the wrong idea from watching television. Why, you might think cops have to tell you what the charge is, read you your rights, things like that."

Toothy folded his arms and didn't say anything.

"I've thought about it," I said, "and I've decided you guys would have more friends if you'd stop that incessant jabbering."

When we got to the Dalton County Courthouse, they parked in a ten-space lot at the back and kept us in the cars. A gaggle of kids on BMX bikes rode past, grinning and pointing. Hawkins entered the building through a metal door marked Sheriff's Officers Only. Ten minutes later, he stuck his head out the same door and beckoned to the deputies waiting with us. We all went inside that time.

Edson's office was bright and airy, with light wood paneling. Edson sat in a leather chair behind a tidy blond desk. Hawkins and Toothy marched us up to the desk, then retreated to stand against the wall. Edson tapped his forefinger on his blotter and said, "Empty your pockets, boys. Pile it all right here."

I took my investigator's license out of my wallet and laid it on top of the polaroids of Vivian and the bikers. I put the rest of my pocket junk in a separate pile.

"Those pictures are evidence in a pending criminal case, Sheriff. Lieutenant Edward Durkee in Dallas is waiting for them."

Cowboy unloaded, too. He grinned savagely as he took a gigantic folding knife from his left boot and ever-so-gently put it on top of his pile.

Edson looked at the knife and shot Hawkins a glance that threatened to amend the night-time roster for the next three months.

Up close, Edson didn't look quite so heroic. He had a bald spot. His lips were a touch too thin and his ruddy complexion seemed to owe more to empty bottles than the Texas sun.

Edson put Cowboy's knife in a desk drawer. He handed my license to Hawkins with a sour look. "Check that out."

He slowly and carefully examined our personal gear, then quickly leafed through the amateur porno pictures.

Finally, he leaned back in his chair, folded his hands on his stomach, and scowled at me.

"Okay, Mr. Big Shot Private Detective from Dallas, I want to hear how you manage to get into so much trouble so fast. You been in my county for three days. So far, I got a motel burned down, with a barbecued body in what used to be your room. I got Bart Dolan's kid shooting off his mouth about motorcycle gangs. I got a prominent businessman shot full of .22s and I find you two holed up with enough firepower to—"

"Excuse me, Sheriff. What's that about someone shot with a .22?"

"You're really making my day, city boy. I suppose you're going to pretend you don't know nothing about that."

"I don't."

"You spent most of yesterday hanging around his office, you just got caught in a house he owns, and you're telling me you didn't know T. J. MacCready got himself killed this morning?"

"Hoo-boy," said Cowboy.

"Well, Sheriff," I said, "let's talk about that."

CHAPTER TWENTY-EIGHT

Sheriff Edson put his photogenic chin down on his chest and looked up through his white eyebrows while I told him about Vivian Mollison and her sale to the bikers. After the first five minutes, he opened a desk drawer and took four seconds too long to bring his hand out with a long cigar in it.

He unwrapped the cigar, he rolled it around in the flame from a kitchen match, he inhaled deeply, and he let a blue cloud of smoke drift across the desk top.

It smelled wonderful.

I said, "So, I had the old reports that mentioned Conover as either a name or a town, Sheriff. When I heard about a shooting at a Dallas beer joint and found out the bikes involved had plates stolen in Dalton County, it seemed logical to come out here. You'd have done the same thing."

Edson sucked his cigar and silently rejected my offer to compare investigative techniques. Hawkins came in with my license and whispered in Edson's ear.

"I identified myself to your dispatcher on Monday," I said, "when I got Billy Dolan's name as the owner of the stolen plate."

Edson waved his cigar at Hawkins. Hawkins left the office again.

"I also had to check out the responses from a newspaper ad asking for information about biker activity. Maybe you saw it. The ad had my Dallas phone number in it." I told him about Arbetha Fullylove and how MacCready used the bikers to pressure her.

"Seems to me, you're working up an excuse for killing MacCready," Edson said.

"Wrong, Sheriff. I'm telling you why I wanted to *talk* to him. We couldn't find him. So we cruised the area looking for bikers. Saw a big Harley leaving that farm house where you found us, but he got away on a back road. Then—after they tried to french-fry us at the motel—we went to the farm house looking for them. Well, they weren't there, of course, only the girl. We found those pictures, though, which proved we had the right place. So we waited for them to come back. You came, instead."

"That's it?" Edson said around the cigar.

"Sure. What more could there be?"

"Oh, I dunno, exactly. Maybe there could be a part about how you ran MacCready off the road near the motel, took him to his office, and killed him when he wouldn't tell you what you wanted to hear. Or maybe you shot him out of pure cussedness. You tell me."

"What time was that supposed to have happened?"

Edson blew smoke at the ceiling. "Eight o'clock, give or take," he said. "That's only preliminary, of course. Doc might fine it down some later."

"No problem," I said. "Talk to the waitress at that cafe across from the Ford place outside Conover. We ate breakfast there. And Thun—uh, the girl at the biker place can tell you when we got there. It couldn't have been more than ten minutes after we left the cafe."

"Time of death could be off a mite," Edson said. "Maybe you shot MacCready, then went to eat."

"You're smarter than that, Sheriff. Hell, it's staring you in the face. You said MacCready was killed with a .22. I bet that's not quite right. I bet they were .223 slugs. From military M16s. Neither of us carries anything even close to that caliber. You might find some buried in the motel woodwork, though, if the damage wasn't complete. And the bikers left a box of M16 ammo at the house. The girl showed me.''

''And you don't know these bikers by name?''

''No idea, Sheriff. I should have thought to ask the girl.''

Hawkins came back into the office. He nodded at Edson. The sheriff puffed on that glorious cigar for a few minutes, then said, ''Gonna take a while to check out all this bullshit, you know.''

''Fine,'' I said. ''Take your time. Your jail food any good?''

''Ain't won no awards lately, but it won't kill you. Hawkins.''

Hawkins front-and-centered, fishing jail keys out of his pocket.

''Lock 'em up,'' Edson said. He removed two dollars from my wallet and handed them to Hawkins. ''And get Rafferty some cigarettes. He's gonna hurt his insides, sucking up second-hand smoke like that.''

''Won't kill you, my ass,'' Cowboy said. He put his half-eaten plate of rice and beans on the concrete floor outside our cell and settled back on the lower bunk. He sipped from the cup of green Kool-Aid that completed the two-course dinner at the county jail Hilton.

Edson's jail wasn't so bad, as county jails go. It was clean, the bunks had mattresses on them, and the disinfectant smell was a shade below overpowering. And it certainly wasn't crowded. We were the only occupants in the cell block.

Cowboy was right about the food, though.

''Look,'' I said, ''we'll be out of here soon. If Edson was seriously fitting us out for the MacCready killing, he'd have had us strip-searched, booked, and sprayed, all those welcome home gestures.''

''Maybe,'' said Cowboy. ''On the other hand, there were a few holes in that story you told him.''

''I didn't hear you come up with anything better.''

Cowboy shrugged. "You did all right, I guess. I wonder how they found MacCready."

"The bikers or the cops?"

"Either."

"Beats me," I said. I lit another cigarette. That was my third in five years. They tasted funny and they were unsatisfying after pipe tobacco. They didn't last very long, either.

But they didn't go out all the time.

"Maybe the bikers went home," Cowboy said. "The girl coulda lied about that. And if MacCready found himself a phone, he might have called them."

"Maybe. Sheriff said MacCready got it in his office. He could have called the bikers in to chew them out."

"And they did the chewing?" Cowboy said.

"It's possible. If so, they know we're not dead."

"Yeah," he said. "But it won't take many more meals like that one."

The lights went out at 10:00. At 10:40, they came on again. Hawkins unlocked the cell door and led us back to Edson's office.

The sheriff looked harried. He scratched his bald spot and growled around another cigar, "Anything you want to add to that cock-and-bull story you told me?"

"No."

"Tell me again. I must be getting old. I forget the good parts."

I went through it again, and ended with, "Play back the tape in your drawer, Sheriff. See if it doesn't sound the same."

"Smart bastard." He didn't look like an election poster sheriff now; he looked like a tired old man.

"All right," he said. "Here's the way she shapes up. You boys were in the cafe. 'Bout half of Conover saw you, I'd say. As to when you got to the Prescott place, I wouldn't believe that Billings kid if she swore it was daylight at noon, but Wiley Lanier was plowing this morning. He seen you two show up when you said you did."

"I hate to say I told you so, Sheriff, but—"

Edson waved his hand angrily and choked on his cigar. When he could talk again, he said, "Watch your smart mouth, Rafferty. I can find something to put you away for, if . . . Aw, hell, forget it. Thing is, a feller working on the pump at Reservoir Three picked up MacCready. Gave him a ride into town and dropped him at his office at exactly 7:15. On top of all that, Hawkins found a silly old bitch who lives behind MacCready's office. She says she heard shots about eight, but thought it was kids setting off *firecrackers*, for cryin' in an old bucket!"

Edson used his cigar to jab at the air between us. "You boys might not have shot MacCready, but that sure as hell don't make us old pals. You attract trouble like a cowpat draws flies. I want you back here for the inquest, course, but until then, I want you out of my face! Now, you two high-binders get your guns and your pocket stuff from the deputy on the counter; you get into that beat-up car out back and you get your lucky asses out of my county!"

Rafferty's Rule Thirty-three: Always obey your friend the policeman.

We got our lucky asses out of Edson's county.

CHAPTER TWENTY-NINE

"I think they're gone," I told Hilda and Fran over breakfast. "Split. Vamoosed. Cut out for Canada or Mexico or Williamsburg, Virginia."

"Williamsburg, Virginia?" Fran said. She speared an egg yolk with a toast triangle.

"Well, gone, anyway."

Hilda topped up my coffee and said, "You look terrible, big guy."

"I feel worse than that. We got back about three. Cowboy went home. He's still worried about a new foal. I would have slept in, except I wanted to get over here and see my girls."

Hilda smiled. "One of your girls has a new job."

Fran grinned hugely. "How about that? Two-twenty a week and I don't have to take off my clothes or hustle drinks or anything."

"Congratulations," I said. "When do you start?"

"Monday. Which reminds me. It's time for me to move out of here."

"Oak Cliff to Richardson is a helluva commute every day," I said. "You must like buses."

"Listen to this," Fran said. "There's a studio apartment only four blocks from the shop and Hilda loaned me the deposit and can you help me cart stuff over there this afternoon?''

I looked at Hilda. She winked at me. "The kid bugs me. I wanted to get rid of her."

"Ho, ho," Fran chortled. "Your oven will never be so clean again. She's being sweet, Rafferty. One day, I'll have a job selling antiques for her."

"We'll see," Hilda said. "Stranger things have happened."

"Stranger people have never happened," I said. "Fran, you should see some of the neuters she—"

"Come on!" said Hilda. "It's not them, it's you! I think you scare them."

"I'll settle for that. Fran, let's move you tomorrow. I promised to take you to the cops today."

I told her about Ed Durkee and said, "You might not have to testify for a long time, if at all. This is just a final detail for both of us. I'm out of it now. The cops can do a better job from here on. If nothing else, Dixon and Lockhart will get picked up after a traffic ticket in Utah."

"What happened to Virginia?"

"Whatever."

"Do I have to talk to the police?"

"Yep. I said you would and you owe me."

Hilda bristled. "That's pretty bald, Rafferty!"

"He's right," Fran said. She wiped her lips and folded her napkin. "I owe it to him. And it's the right thing to do. So, sir, let's go for it, before I lose my nerve."

Fran cleared the dishes away and went off to change.

Women dress up for the damnedest things. Me, I planned to go the way I was. My jeans were nearly new and my polo shirt hadn't shrunk yet. Much, anyway.

After Fran left the kitchen, Hilda and I sat at the table, holding hands and smiling at each other. When five minutes passed and we hadn't said anything, Fran called from her bedroom, "Break it up, you two! That's a clean tablecloth."

* * *

I introduced Fran to Durkee and Ricco. She surprised them both, I think. Perhaps they expected a gum-cracking punk rocker in oily leathers.

Ed trotted out the lugubrious formality he saved for the clean-living half of the public. Ricco smarmed all over Fran, but didn't quite bring it off. Usually, he acted like a pimp. This time, he behaved more like a burial plot salesman.

I gave Ed the photos, and showed him which one was Turk and which one I thought was Smokey Joe. He carefully held his big thumbs over the naughty parts when he asked Fran to confirm my opinions. Then the pictures went into the file.

"*That's* why I can't run my business like you real cops," I said. "I can't afford so many file cabinets."

I told Fran I had another stop to make and offered her cab fare.

"No, thanks," she said. "Depending on when I finish here, I might meet Hilda for lunch. Or I'll window-shop until she's ready to go home." She reached for my hand and squeezed it. "I'm fine now. Go on."

"Okay."

I gave Ed and Ricco a Dutch uncle look. "No rubber hoses, you clowns. This is a friend of mine."

Ed looked pained. Ricco didn't get it.

When I went out the door, Fran was holding her head high and carefully explaining Holman, Zifretti, et al. She looked terrific; self-assured and content with herself.

The DA had a big problem, I decided. He would never convince a jury Fran had once run with a motorcycle gang.

On the way out to the Mollisons, I wondered if I could afford to retire the Mustang. I still owed Cowboy two day's wages; there hadn't been enough cash to pay him in full. Cowboy was an expense account item, though, as were motel bills, gas, wear, and tear . . . Also, Mollison owed me another three thousand dollars for the biker in the Conover court fire. So call it an even four thousand.

I could afford to replace the Mustang with another car. Not a new one, of course, but why would I want a new car? Old ones are so much easier to throw away.

In that frame of mind, I wheeled into Mollison's driveway, sauntered to the front door, and punched the button. I dug out my new pipe—a short-stemmed Falcon—and loaded it while I eyed the rusty Mustang and imagined its replacement.

I had my head down, lighting the pipe, when the door opened. I turned, ready for one of Consuela's thousand-watt smiles.

It wasn't Consuela, though. Or Marge or George or even Vivian.

It was Smokey Joe Lockhart.

With an M16 in his hands and an evil grin on his thick lips.

I rushed him, and pushed the flaring gas lighter into his face. The M16's flame arrestor gashed my arm as I shoved the muzzle aside and tried for a knee thrust to his groin.

He howled, mostly from surprise and fright at the flames licking his beard, I thought. I did pretty well at first. Smokey Joe was my weight, near enough, and shorter. And he was backed into a wall, which held him up. I dropped the lighter, grabbed hair and ears in each hand, and made a very good attempt to pound the back of his head through the wall.

It wasn't quite good enough. A heavy object the size of Omaha slammed into the angle where my neck met my left shoulder. My left side stopped working. Omaha landed on my back next, and after that, the side of my neck again.

Smokey Joe drifted away, or maybe I did. It didn't seem important at the time.

There were hoarse shouts in the background, and a woman screamed somewhere, high and piercing and plaintive. There was a lot of scuffling, but I didn't pay much attention, because I was face down on the carpet, with my nose painfully splayed to one side. Nothing below my neck worked.

I thought and thought, but no matter how hard I tried, I couldn't come up with a single rule to cover that situation.

CHAPTER THIRTY

One of the disadvantages of being big is that, after losing a fight, there is so much of you to hurt.

I'll be fair. Small people must have problems with fights, too. Presumably, they hurt more often.

When I decided I wasn't going to lose consciousness again, no matter how attractive that sounded, I opened my eyes. It was a room I hadn't seen before, though apparently still in the Mollison house.

I was seated—slumped, actually—on a sofa. There was another sofa on the opposite side of a glass-topped coffee table.

Turk Dixon was seated on the other sofa.

"Does this mean you don't want to buy an encyclopedia?" I said.

Turk didn't say anything and neither did anyone else, although there were other people in the room. I knew they were there and I wanted to see them. I shook my head to clear my vision. That was a lousy idea.

After a long woozy spell, I tried turning my head slowly and blinking. That worked better.

The room was a study. Not a real study, in the precise meaning of the term. It was one of those studies where the interior decorator ordered books by the color of the binding and the length of the shelf.

The room was long and narrow. The sofa grouping was at one end, near the only door. The other end of the room housed a huge leather-topped desk with a judge's chair behind it and bookshelves behind that. The wall I faced—the one behind Turk's sofa—had a fireplace in the middle and bay windows on each side.

The windows looked out over the Mollison front yard, the whole half acre of it. It was bright and sunny and inviting out there. A silver Mercedes silently oozed down the distant street.

People. Who were those people again? Turk, of course. And Smokey Joe Lockhart, sitting on the sofa beside Turk. And Vivian of the blank look standing beside the sofa, naked and skinny and uncomplaining as Turk idly twined his fingers in her pubic hair.

Something wet and cold dabbed at my arm. I jumped.

"It's all right," Marge Mollison said. She wiped again at the gouge on my forearm. She stuck an adhesive bandage over the wound and pressed it down harder than was necessary.

Marge wore a white summery dress. It was badly wrinkled. There were perspiration stains under her arms. And she was still hot.

"Where the hell have you been?" she said. "Do you have any idea what we've been going through for the last day and night, waiting for you to show up?"

"Damned inconsiderate, Rafferty," George Mollison's voice boomed. "Whatever happened to customer service?"

I finally found him, slouched in the chair behind the desk. He had a Scotch bottle in one hand and a full glass in the other.

"Remember what you said, Rafferty? 'I can't quit,' you said. 'I'll get them whether you want me to or not!' Wasn't that your high-sounding little speech?"

George waved his bottle arm in an exaggerated gesture at Turk and Smokey Joe. "Well, there they are, Rafferty. Go get 'em!"

I refocused on Marge. It hurt. "What happened?"

"Consuela answered the door yesterday, during lunch. They barged in."

"Have they hurt any of you?"

Marge shook her head in a tight, controlled movement. "None of us got shot, if that's what you mean. That one," she nodded toward Turk, "raped Vivian last night."

"Rape? You can't rape Skinny Mama, lady. She loves it. Don't you, baby?" He smirked at Vivian, then winked at me. "Taught her myself."

Turk was fortyish and well built for a biker. He was bare-chested under his denim vest. He wore black jeans and heavy leather boots with chains riveted onto them. He had olive skin and, with his shaved head and an upward tilt to his eyes, he looked vaguely Oriental. On his lap, he had an M16 with the fire selector on automatic.

On the other end of the sofa, Smokey Joe had his M16 pointed at me. He seemed to want an excuse to use it.

Smokey Joe was chubby and dirty and hairy. His clothes were similar to Turk's, except he wore a dark green T-shirt under his vest and he had a broad flat-brimmed black hat with a snakeskin band. He also had an ugly blister on his cheek and his right eye watered continually. Every few moments, he wiped away the tears with the back of a hammy hand.

"Okay, Turk," I said. "What's the play?"

"Oh, that's good," he said. " 'What's the play, Turk?' *Big man*. The play, you asshole, is this. Ever since Skinny Mama's folks hired you, we had nothing but trouble. Brothers been dying, man, and I take that serious. By rights, I should off you now, but I tell you what I'm gonna do. Since it ain't personal, since you're just a hired man, we won't go to war over it."

When Smokey Joe didn't have any objections to me remaining unpunished, I put Turk's generous offer in the same category as 'I'm from the government and I'm here to help you.'

Turk said, "Smoke and I, we're gonna take off soon. Skinny Mama will come with us." He glanced at Marge to see what reaction he got.

Marge flinched, then stared at him coldly.

Turk guffawed, then he turned to me. "The way I figure it, Skinny Mama's folks know if you give us any more trouble, Mama ain't getting another free ticket home."

He leered up at Vivian. "Right, Mama? Your folks fuck up, you're dog meat, baby."

Vivian stood placidly and watched the wall. Turk slapped her flank the way you would slap a horse of which you were moderately fond.

"So," Turk said to me, "you're out of a job, pal. Your employment contract has been severed." He pronounced it *see-vered*. "You got that straight?"

"Got it," I said. I stood up. Smokey Joe's M16 followed me. "My back is killing me. Got to loosen up."

"Hey, go ahead," Turk said. "We're all buddies here. Loosen up. Be cool."

I stretched and twisted and paced toward the desk end of the long room. I said, "All you want from me is my word I'll lay off. Is that right?"

"Well, almost all."

I nodded thoughtfully. "That's no problem. No future in this gig, anyway."

"That's my man!" Turk said. "So, okay, we got that part straightened out. There's only one other small problem. That Zifretti bitch, the one you took away from us at the strip joint."

I reached the desk and turned. George looked up, then dove back into his Scotch glass.

I stretched again, shook my legs, and walked back toward the sofas.

"The Zifretti cunt," Turk said. "She knows more than she should. And she's got a big mouth. Now, *you* I understand. No pay, no play, right? But Tony's old lady talks too much. That's bad for everybody. She talked to her brother-in-law and look what happened to him."

I reached the sofas and passed behind the one where I had awakened.

"So what about her?" I said as I got to the end of the room and turned to face Turk.

"That's the other part," Turk said. "I want her. I want to know where she is right now."

"Oh, hell, Turk, I can do better than that. I'll go get her for you."

Then I opened the door and stepped out of the room.

CHAPTER THIRTY-ONE

No one expected me to simply walk out. As I closed the study door, there were muffled curses. A heavy piece of furniture thumped onto the floor.

I surprised myself when I beat the bikers out of the house. I reached the Mustang and had the glove compartment open before either of them reached the front steps.

I surprised Smokey Joe even more. When he skidded out the front door, I was waiting with the .45 in my fist. I shot him in the face. He fell head down on the steps and leaked onto the flagstone walk.

Turk came out next. His brain was already catching up to his legs; he was backpedaling frantically when he appeared. He pulled back out of sight as I squeezed the trigger again.

A cast iron carriage lamp by the front door exploded. Part of the metal frame landed on Smokey Joe's back. It looked like a black hand with two thumbs.

I grabbed the second clip for the .45 from the glove compartment and shoved it into my hip pocket. Then, as fast as my aching legs would let me, I ran along the front of the house looking for the study window.

The sill was too high to let me see the whole room, but I recognized the wallpaper. I slapped the window glass. It shivered. I held the .45 in both hands and waited to see whose face would appear.

Marge Mollison, with her mouth in an elongated O.

I pantomimed throwing something through the glass and stepped aside. Twenty seconds later, a floor lamp with an ornate base sailed out the window and made a manhole-sized depression in the lawn.

When glass stopped falling, I raked the .45 barrel over the jagged edges on the sill and yelled, "Come on! Get out of there!"

Marge had to help George through. He sat on the sill, wavered, and fell heavily when she pushed him out. He tumbled onto his side. Marge stepped on the sill and jumped. The light material of her dress floated up around her waist as she dropped to the ground. She wore pretty sexy underwear for such an icy personality.

"Where's Vivian?" I asked.

"He dragged Vivian out of the room," Marge said. "I don't know where they went."

"Consuela?"

"They told her to make sandwiches, but that was quite a while ago."

I pointed at George, who was trying to stand up and doing a lousy job of it. "Get him out of here!"

She prodded him down the front lawn toward the street; a slender white-uniformed nanny herding a surly youngster.

I went back toward the front door, keeping close to the house and trying to remember the layout of the interior.

I could have waited for the cops, of course. They're pretty good at prying out armed suspects. The trouble was, Turk had two hostages: a blonde zombie in whom I had a big stake and a gentle brown girl with a smile that shouldn't be wasted.

Besides, where does it say you can live forever?

I went through the front door in a rolling rush and came up hard against the wall where I had fought with Smokey Joe. There was no blurt of automatic fire. I waited, sweating, and listened to the house.

An air-conditioning duct purred somewhere. A wind chime tinkled on the back patio, barely audible through the glass doors. There was another sound, too, like a small wounded animal, but I couldn't be sure from where it came.

I put my head around the wall down low, at floor level. The living room furniture was hi-tech, too spindly to conceal anyone. When I crossed the room, the animal sound was louder.

It took me several minutes to check a short hallway to the right off the living room. The first door was a walk-in linen closet. Empty. The second door was a guest bathroom. Empty.

The third was the master bedroom. Almost empty. I nearly blew a calico cat into fur balls when it suddenly hopped onto the bed.

The adjoining bathroom was empty. The cat was asleep when I went back through the bedroom.

I retraced my steps down the short hall and crossed the living room. A whoop-whoop of distant sirens drifted in through the open front door.

I went through a formal dining room quickly, then spent a long time beside the archway leading to the kitchen.

The animal sound came from the kitchen proper. There was something behind the long serving counter. The sound was like a rabbit being squeezed every other second; a back-of-the-throat reflex laced with hysteria.

There was only one way to do it. I took two short steps, belly-flopped onto the counter and stuck my head—and the .45—over the far edge.

Consuela, alone and terrified, stared up into the gun. It must have looked like a sewer pipe to her.

She sat on the floor, huddled into a corner with her round brown knees drawn up. She had her thumb knuckle jammed between her strong white teeth. A thin trail of blood dribbled down her chin and dripped onto the bodice of her uniform.

I slid off the counter, tugged her upright, and took her into the living room. When I pointed her at the front door, she took off in a fluid canter and didn't look back.

The sirens were louder now and there were more of them.

The only unexplored territory was a long hallway that ran down the back of the house. There were bedrooms to the left, I thought, probably with a bathroom or two in between. To the right, glass doors alternated with white brick walls that had paintings hung on them.

Near the head of the hallway, there was an oval antique table with a delicate china bowl on it. I slid the bowl down the hall as hard as I could. When it wobbled into a room at the far end, a burst of eight rounds shattered it and chewed up the gold carpet.

That solved the first problem. I knew where he was.

Now for the hard part.

"Rafferty?" he yelled. "Back off now or I'll blow Skinny Mama's head open like a punkin, man."

"She'd never know it, Turk. You killed her a long time ago."

He kept yelling about what he would do if I didn't let him leave the house. I used the noise as cover and scuttled down the hallway. I passed other bedrooms and baths, then stopped outside the end room, where he was holed up.

He quit yelling. I waited and listened.

I wondered how to enter the room. The book—for those who believe in the book—says you should run four or five steps into the room, turn and fire. The theory is based on the trapped man expecting you to stick your head around the corner.

That method works most of the time. Every once in a while, though, you run across someone who read the same book.

"Tough luck, asshole," Turk's voice said softly.

Behind me?

Oh, my sweet Christ, he came out through an adjoining bathroom!

I turned just enough to see his sweating bald head and sneering grin and the matt-finished M16 in his hands.

Then a yellow egg flew out of the forgotten bathroom and smashed into Turk's face. Blood sprayed from his nose. He nearly dropped the M16 as he pulled the trigger.

The noise in the narrow space was loud, hurtful to the ears. Something like a brick slapped my right ankle—all pressure, no pain—and I fell on my right side with my head toward Turk.

He had dropped to his knees. The egg hit him again, retreated on a white tail, and came back to bounce off the back of his head with a dull *thonk*!

The muzzle of Turk's M16 rested on the light-colored carpet. His head lolled. He leaned forward over the gun like a Muslim at prayer. I could have touched his cheek.

Turk raised his head, shook it, and focused on me. He lifted his torso slightly, hugged the M16 to his chest, and ponderously swayed to point the muzzle at my stomach. His right hand scrabbled like a demented spider copulating with the M16 handgrip and trigger.

I stretched as far as I could, put the .45 against his neck, and pulled the trigger twice.

The blasts reverberated through the house. A painting fell off the wall. It was small, hardly bigger than a large index card. There was a lot of blue in it.

Vivian stepped out of the bathroom. She had a thick white cord wrapped around one wrist. It was a loop, with a cake of yellow soap formed around one end.

I looked up at her and tried to grin. "I get it," I croaked. "The old soap-on-a-rope trick."

She let the loop slide off her wrist and held out her hands to me. I took them and she helped me sit up, then lean against the wall.

The change of position started a rush of pain in my ankle. There wasn't much blood yet, but the holes did not look promising.

I began to sweat like a pig. At the same time, I felt cold and clammy.

Vivian knelt on the floor beside me. She put her hands on my cheeks and turned my head to face her. She peered intently at me from six inches away. There was something in her eyes I had not seen before.

"I know you," she said. "Hi, Mr. Rafferty."

Then she sat facing me and took my trembling sweaty hands in her cool dry ones.

We were sitting like that, both of us crying softly, when the first uniformed squad arrived.

ABOUT THE AUTHOR

W. Glenn Duncan, a former newsman, politician, and
professional pilot, has lived in Iowa, Ohio, Oregon,
Florida, Texas, and California. He now lives with his
wife and three children in Australia. RAFFERTY'S
RULES is his first novel.

A Special Blend...

MYSTERY, ADVENTURE and THE WORLD of RACING

DICK FRANCIS

12   TAF-19